AUBURN AVENUE

By

D.L. Jordan

"I have the nerve to walk my own way, however hard, in my search for reality, rather than climb upon the rattling wagon of wishful illusions."

— **Zora Neale Hurston**

TABLE OF CONTENTS

PROLOGUE

Atlanta, Georgia. Monday, July 3, 1911.

A somber hush lay draped over the city like a funeral cloth, suffocating even the memory of life that had danced through the streets only hours earlier. It was the kind of quiet that didn't just settle, it gripped. Heavy and unnatural, it pressed into every corner, every windowpane, every gutter, as though the city itself were mourning some unspoken loss. The air, thick with heat and the residue of the day, felt

1

too dense to breathe freely. It clung to skin, to walls, to rooftops, as if hoping to preserve the last traces of something already gone.

The night was not kind. It was not gentle in its descent. It was swollen, tense, and humid, holding on with the brittle grip of something nearing its end, like an old man in his final hours, unwilling to slip away, yet no longer strong enough to hold on. Above, the stars hung faintly behind a gauzy shroud of haze, as though reluctant to witness what lay beneath. The moon, dulled and waning, resembled a ghost of its former self, more memory than light. It offered neither guidance nor grace, merely a pale reflection of something greater that had long since passed.

Atlanta, once so quickened by the clatter of footsteps and streetcars, the call-and-response of sidewalk preachers and poets, now held its breath. The city, with its brick bones and iron joints, seemed to forget how to breathe. Along Auburn Avenue, that proud artery of Black enterprise and spirit, silence took up residence where sound had once ruled. The perfume of bourbon, of sweet perfume and sweat, the scent of stories told in between the bars of ragtime, vanished. The warm glow from club windows

2

had given way to cold neon flicker, each sign buzzing weakly as though unsure if it should continue trying.

Barrooms that only hours ago had echoed with laughter now stood still, shuttered and mute beneath hand-painted signs. Inside, the ghosts of celebration lingered, half-drunk bottles, lipstick on tumblers, a chair askew, but even they seemed exhausted. Where once piano keys danced and voices harmonized in messy, glorious defiance of sorrow, now only the occasional creak of a settling floorboard dared to speak.

And then, from the veins of this silenced body of a city, a pulse: movement in an alleyway too narrow for anything but secrecy. Its brick walls bore the long story of time, blackened by smoke, chipped by weather, and slick with the residue of rain that hadn't touched the ground in days. In that cramped corridor between buildings, a figure emerged, not with the clumsiness of panic or the aimlessness of a wanderer, but with the measured certainty of one who belonged to the shadows.

The gas lamp overhead, crooked on its rusted mount, hissed and spat against the night. Its flame trembled, erratic, barely clinging to life.

And yet, in that tremble was enough light to catch the glint of polished leather, the crisp edges of wool pressed to sharp seams. The man beneath the light did not flinch. His movement was slow, exacting, like that of someone for whom every gesture had been rehearsed to perfection. A coat, long, impeccably tailored, clung to his frame with an air of understated elegance. Gloves, smooth and black as ink, covered hands that might once have held softer things, or deadlier.

His hat, wide-brimmed and angled just so — was not fashion but intention. It denied the night any glimpse of the eyes beneath, the thoughts they might betray, or the past they might reveal. His face, what little of it the dim light allowed, remained a cipher. At the alley's midpoint he paused, leaning against the wall in silence. He did not fidget or sigh or scan the horizon. He simply became part of the brick and the hush, his breath so even it seemed not to exist at all.

Then, with the kind of ease that suggests familiarity bordering on ritual, he reached into his coat and retrieved a cigarette. It moved to his lips like a final word spoken in confidence. The match, when it struck, flared with a soft hiss, a brief rebellion against the quiet. It cracked the air, not loud, but definite, like a warning or a promise. In that flare, just for a heartbeat, his jaw became visible. Firm. Angular. Unspeaking.

Then darkness claimed the moment again, and only the ember of the cigarette remained, glowing faintly in the cradle of his breath — a tiny orange eye in the dark.

A sound, a subtle, rhythmic tapping — broke his stillness. Not loud, but persistent. Too intentional to be the wind, too steady to be coincidence. It echoed faintly off the narrow brick walls, a cadence that didn't belong to the night's hush.

Footsteps.

His body responded before his mind had the chance to form a thought. The tension rose through him like a wire pulled taut. The cigarette, once lazily perched at the corner of his mouth, sagged unnoticed. His hand, calm but decisive, disappeared into the folds of his coat. Fingers curled with practiced familiarity around the cold metal nestled in the lining, a pistol, worn in places from use, but dependable. Trustworthy. Deadly.

He didn't breathe. He didn't blink. Every muscle coiled with restrained energy as his eyes, shadowed beneath the brim of his hat, locked on the alley's entrance. The footsteps were louder now. Slower. Less a march than a message, deliberate, unhurried, the sound of someone who knew they were being watched and came anyway.

Then, as if conjured from the dark, the silhouette of another man materialized.

He didn't speak at first. He didn't need to. The lines of his frame, the elegance of his coat, the tilt of his hat — all familiar. Still, the first man did not relax. Suspicion hung thick between the walls, suspended in the moisture-heavy air. But the second man raised both hands slowly, palms out, fingers spread inside leather gloves that caught the flickering gaslight just enough to reflect honesty — or at least the performance of it.

"Hold on!" the second man called softly. His voice slid through the alley like a scalpel — precise, smooth, undeniably present. It had a quality that demanded pause without begging for it. "It's only me."

For a heartbeat, long, dense, electric, nothing moved. The first man didn't speak. Didn't lower his arm. The sound of silence stretched like a blade drawn from its sheath.

Then, with the discipline of a soldier disarming after the signal, the first man exhaled — slow, controlled, almost soundless. His fingers uncurled from the pistol's grip and withdrew from the pocket without fanfare. He didn't show the weapon. He didn't need to. The threat had spoken clearly in posture alone.

"Don't do that again," he muttered, the cigarette bobbing slightly with the motion of his lips. The words came out like gravel pressed through cloth — quiet but rough. "I could've killed you."

"Not if I had gotten to you first," the second man replied, stepping into the alley with a fluid grace. His shoes tapped against the damp cobblestone, the sound muted by the night's moisture. His voice lacked arrogance but not confidence. It was the tone of someone who spoke not in challenge, but in fact.

They faced each other in the space between two worlds — light and dark, known and unknown. There was no smile. No shared history in their expressions. Only the brittle bond of necessity. Men who had been strangers until a need had stitched them together like sutures on a wound.

Their exchange bore no warmth, no sentiment. Not even the brittle comfort of mutual respect. What passed between them was the language of consequence — the kind forged under pressure and sealed in silence.

"So, are we still in agreement?" the first man asked, his voice clipped and quiet, his gaze never leaving the second figure. His question wasn't casual. It was a checkpoint, a locked door waiting for a key.

The second man nodded once, a gesture barely perceptible in the low light. "Just as long as you hold up your end of the bargain."

A long pause followed — heavier than words, weighted with what wasn't being said.

"Oh, don't you worry about that," the first man said at last. A faint shift curled into his voice — a tendril of something darkly amused, confidently coiled. "Rest assured, you will have your money once the task is complete."

"Good," the other replied, simple and final.

Another silence crept in, this one different — colder, flatter. Like the space before an executioner gives the signal.

"She'll be out of our lives soon," the first man said, and his tone held no hesitation, no regret. Only the solid finality of intent laid bare.

What followed was not just quiet — it was an absence, a vacuum. The kind of stillness that comes just after the last shovelful of earth falls on a coffin. No response came. None was needed. Agreement had been forged in the shadows long before this night arrived.

They reached for each other's hands, not like old friends or brothers, but like businessmen sealing a contract they hoped never to revisit. The handshake was brief, tight, without ceremony. No witnesses. No need.

In that clasp, something passed, not an object, but understanding. A promise. A threat. A shared burden dressed in opportunity.

Then, with the brevity of those who know time is not on their side, they separated.

No goodbye. No nod. Just movement.

One turned left. The other right. Two silhouettes retreating into the dark veins of a city pretending to sleep. Behind them, only the echo of footsteps remained, fading like memories.

And the ember of a cigarette, smoldering in the gutter, whispering the only truth that night had room to hold.

CHAPTER 1

JACK

The morning broke not in a rush, but in elegance, unfurling slowly like a ribbon of gold draped across the sleeping silhouette of the city. Light filtered through the architecture of old brick and new ambition, pouring like honey between the narrow gaps of rising buildings and casting soft warmth onto the cobblestone streets below. The air was rich with the scent of fresh earth, soot, and summer dew, blended into that unmistakable perfume of a city just beginning to stir.

It was the Fourth of July, and even before the crowds, the speeches, or the fireworks, something in the atmosphere had changed. The day carried its own heartbeat, pulsing with a kind of anticipation. A hum. A vibration. As though the city itself was holding its breath—not out of fear, but expectancy.

Even in these early hours, Auburn Avenue was awake.

The street pulsed with motion and melody. Horse-drawn carriages clattered rhythmically over the uneven stones, the iron rims of their wheels striking the ground in a metallic cadence. Their hooves echoed in neat, staccato bursts as uniformed coachmen guided them through the waking thoroughfare, the sharp crack of leather reins occasionally breaking the morning's lull. The harness bells jingled not just out of utility, but as if they were part of the city's own symphony—each chime adding to the growing harmony of dawn.

Electric streetcars hummed on their tracks, their bright brass bells ringing out in short, deliberate notes as they moved through intersections. Sparks leapt from overhead lines with an electric hiss, momentarily lighting up the tangle of wires above like miniature fireworks. The scent of ozone clung to the air around them, crisp and modern, a whiff of the future tracing the path of steel wheels.

Here and there, the new age announced itself with the purr and cough of combustion. Automobiles — still novel enough to turn heads, crept alongside the carriages, the two worlds sharing space, not yet colliding. A Ford Model T chugged forward with mechanical determination, its wooden spokes turning beneath a proud black body. A Matheson, sleeker and bolder, glided past it, its polished frame gleaming like liquid obsidian as it caught a stray beam of light.

These machines, with their huffing engines and oil-slicked guts, spoke of what was coming. But they didn't own the streets yet. Not here. Not today.

The sidewalks teemed with early risers — men caught in the flurry of routine and purpose. Laborers in short-sleeves loaded crates onto pushcarts, their hands calloused and efficient. Milk bottles clinked together as they were stacked with care. Firewood thudded softly onto wagons, the scent of pine mingling with dust and

sweat. These were the city's working shoulders —
quiet, sturdy, often overlooked.

Beside them, men dressed in pinstriped
trousers and starched collars walked with
sharper pace and straighter backs. Their polished
shoes tapped in confident rhythm, newspapers
tucked beneath their arms, briefcases swinging
slightly at their sides. They exchanged greetings
in passing—nods, tipped hats, murmured
"Mornin', sir." Their movements were
purposeful, but unhurried. Even time itself, on
such a morning, seemed to tip its hat and slow its
step.

On the corner, leaned against the red brick
wall of a tobacconist shop, stood a shoeshine
stand—modest in size, but rich in character. Its
operator, a man bent at the waist and focused
with near-religious intensity, worked his brush in
a rhythm only he could hear. Back and forth. Back
and forth. The bristles rasped against worn
leather, pulling shine from the scuffs, as though
polishing away the sins of yesterday. His sleeves
were rolled, his fingers stained with polish, but
his motion never faltered. Not even when a fine
gentleman above him shifted his weight
impatiently.

The boot, once dull and lifeless, now caught the sun and held it—mirrored it back as if reminding the world that even the streets had their moments of brilliance.

This was Auburn Avenue, not yet dressed for the pageantry to come, but alive in its own quiet majesty. A street breathing history and humming with the weight of footsteps—past, present, and rising fast toward a future no one could quite name yet.

And somewhere, beneath all this movement and murmur, the memory of last night lingered—an unspoken thread winding its way through the city's pulse.

Women moved among them all, gliding like drifting petals through the bustle of Auburn Avenue. They were graceful, serene, and deliberate—figures of quiet elegance weaving through a tapestry of sound and steam. Long dresses whispered along the cobblestones, the hems adorned with lace, ribbons, or neat rows of ruffles that bounced with each careful step. High collars stood proud beneath finely structured jawlines, while silk sashes caught the morning breeze and fluttered like banners from another time.

15

Their hats were architectural marvels — wide-brimmed and adorned with feathers, flowers, and sweeping bows — casting dappled shadows across composed expressions. A few women tilted parasols just so, their delicate wrists bearing the weight with practiced ease. It was protection, yes — but also declaration. Presence. Poise. Pride.

Some led children, small hands wrapped tightly in their own, guiding them through the city's early tempo like a conductor steering a private symphony. Others moved in pairs, their heels clicking in practiced unison, heads bowed together in quiet exchanges of laughter or gossip. Their voices floated into the morning, light and unbothered, fading just beneath the whistle of a distant train or the clang of a shop bell.

And above this living painting — above the motion, the murmurs, the faint scent of roasting peanuts drifting from a vendor's cart — rose the buildings. Compact and weathered, their bricks worn with memory, they stood like sentinels pressed shoulder to shoulder, watching the day begin. Modest apartments perched above storefronts like thoughts above action, each window a glimpse into another heartbeat, another small universe.

Laundry hung like prayer flags from sills and balconies, dresses and shirts swaying gently in the breeze. From open kitchen windows came the clatter of crockery, the sizzle of butter in hot pans, and voices — sleep-tinged, spirited, or still yawning their way into speech. Life was happening here, in quiet pockets and familiar repetitions.

And it was inside one such apartment, on the second floor, nestled in the crook of Auburn Avenue like a warm stone in a rushing stream, that the Franklin household began its own ritual of morning.

The Franklin residence — eleven hundred square feet of modest charm — was not grand, but it breathed with the confidence of a place loved thoroughly. The air was perfumed with cooked grits, warm bread, and the faintest trace of rosemary carried from last night's dinner. Soft light filtered through pale curtains, falling across the floors in buttery streaks and settling like a blessing over every scuffed corner and polished surface.

In the back bedroom, where the light pooled gently across a worn rug and climbed the edge of a cedar wardrobe, Jack Franklin still lay in bed.

African American and forty years old, he was carved by the tools of his trade. Jack was a barber by work, but a craftsman by soul. His hands — broad, capable, and marked with the soft nicks of a thousand careful shaves — rested loosely at his sides, one tucked beneath a pillow still warm with sleep.

His breathing was steady. The sheets were drawn up to his chest, and his brow furrowed now and then as the echo of a dream tickled his consciousness before slipping away. Outside the window, the city called for him. But inside this room, time remained pliant. It stretched around him like the covers he refused to shed.

Beyond the door, in the small but well-kept kitchen-parlor, his wife was already in motion.

Jack's wife, Professor Marion Franklin, an African American woman of forty-one, carried herself with the quiet majesty of someone who had learned to hold a home together with equal parts grace and grit. She was dressed and polished before the hour demanded it, her hair pinned back neatly and her dress smoothed without wrinkle. She did not rush. She orchestrated — her every movement thoughtful, measured, and softly powerful.

Now, standing just beyond the bedroom door, she paused. Arms folded gently, her expression was a blend of affection and amused sternness — the kind that only long love can cultivate. She tilted her head slightly, listening for movement. Nothing. The corners of her mouth lifted.

Raising her knuckles, she gave the door a polite but purposeful knock.

"Jack?" Her voice was light, but held an undertone of challenge. As if daring him to test how long she'd let him linger in bed.

Silence.

She knocked again, this time with just a little more insistence. Her tone shifted — still warm, still teasing — but carrying just enough weight to mean business.

"Jack, are you up yet?"

Still no reply.

Inside the room, Jack stirred. A slow turn beneath the covers. A shuffle. The creak of the mattress. He turned toward the wall, then back again, as if debating whether to return to the fragments of a dream now slipping through his fingers like river water.

A low groan emerged from under the pillow.

"Five more minutes, Marion," he mumbled, voice thick with sleep and stubbornness. There was no real conviction in it—only the practiced protest of a man who knew he would lose the battle, but fought it anyway.

The door creaked open an inch.

Marion stepped inside, her presence like the flick of a switch in a quiet room. The gentle rustle of her skirt accompanied her entrance, and with it came a subtle shift in the air—an energy that was neither hurried nor forceful, but undeniably active. She moved with the grace of repetition, her hands instinctively reaching to straighten the signs of sleep her husband had left behind: a pillow slumped askew, a dog-eared book lying face-down on the floor, its pages slightly crinkled. She set it neatly on the bedside table, adjusted the shade of the lamp so it sat just right, and turned to face him with a look that was equal parts affection and gentle reprimand.

"Not in your life," she said, her voice firm as old oak and just as dependable. Her brow lifted in challenge, but her eyes still held a playful spark.

"You've got to go to work, remember?"

From beneath the covers came a low, dramatic groan. Jack buried his face deeper into the pillow, as though fabric alone could shield him from his wife's logic.

"They can do without me today, I'm sure," came the muffled protest.

Marion's reply was immediate, but never sharp. She wielded discipline the way a skilled pianist touched keys — firm, but with finesse.

"Nonsense. That barbershop isn't going to run itself, you know."

Without warning, she gave the covers a brisk tug, peeling them away in one practiced motion. The morning chill nipped at Jack's skin, drawing a shiver and a groan from him as he curled up momentarily before slowly stretching out again with the stubborn dramatics of a boy forced out of bed for school.

His face emerged from his hands, creased with sleep. He looked like a man who'd wrestled dreams all night and lost. Marion stood at the foot of the bed now, her arms crossed, a smile ghosting at the corners of her mouth.

"Jack, you have to get up. It's already half past seven," she said, a trace of plea in her voice now. "It's the Fourth of July, and those men will want their heads lookin' nice and snazzy for the celebrations tonight."

That line struck something in him. A pause. A flicker of thought behind tired eyes.

Then, slowly, with a groan worthy of an old man and a shake of his head, Jack sat up. The mattress creaked beneath him. He rubbed the back of his neck, then blinked toward the wash table in the corner, where the porcelain basin glimmered faintly in the morning light. Marion must have filled it recently; a thin veil of steam still hovered above the water.

He leaned forward and plunged his hands in, splashing coolness over his face. The shock of it brought him further into the day. His broad fingers moved to the soap dish, lifting the pale bar and working it into a frothy lather. He rubbed his hands and jaw with the muscle memory of routine, efficient, deliberate, unthinking.

Water dripped from his elbows and chin as he paused, blinking again.

"Marion, where'd you place the towels?" he asked, squinting through the haze of his half-wakefulness.

"They're on the rack beside you, dear," she said from across the room, patience layered beneath her tone.

Jack glanced to his left. Sure enough, the towel hung neatly over the small wooden rack, exactly where she'd said. He chuckled, low and sheepish.

"Oh. I see."

Marion laughed, soft and melodic, the sound bouncing lightly off the walls.

"I swear, you'd lose your head if it wasn't attached to you."

Jack grinned, drying his face with the towel, the cotton absorbing not just the water, but the last traces of sleep clinging to him.

"I think you might be right about that," he said.

Behind him, Marion smoothed the quilt with a final, precise tug, then took a step back to admire her work. The bed was neat again, as though night had never touched it. Her hands settled briefly on her hips, and she gave a small nod of

23

satisfaction before turning to him with cheerful resolve.

"Well, all done," she declared. "Now on to the next thing. By the way, breakfast is on the table."

She didn't wait for a reply. With the effortless elegance of a woman whose day was already in full swing, she turned and walked toward the kitchen, her skirt catching the morning air as she moved. The soft click of her heels faded down the hallway.

From the apartment windows, the hum of Atlanta drifted in—voices, wheels on pavement, the distant clatter of a trolley. The scent of cornmeal and warm butter lingered in the air.

And inside the Franklin home, the day had truly begun.

CHAPTER 2

MARION

The warm summer light filtered gently through the narrow windows of the modest Franklin apartment, casting long, soft shadows that stretched and shifted with the slow ascent of the morning sun. Outside, the city thrummed with the restless energy of a new day, but inside these walls, time slowed and softened, folding around the room like a tender embrace. Golden shafts of sunlight spilled over the polished floorboards, warming the pale woven rugs and creeping languidly up the legs of the sturdy oak dining table standing quietly at the center of the parlor.

Though small, the room was suffused with an unmistakable sense of care and quiet dignity that seemed to expand the space beyond its modest dimensions. Every item spoke of intentionality and pride: books neatly lined up on the shelves, polished surfaces catching the light just so, embroidered doilies arranged with fastidious attention, each whispering stories of routine devotion. The parlor served double duty, folding seamlessly into the kitchen. Against the far wall, the cast iron stove still radiated a gentle warmth from the morning's labors, and the rich, savory aroma of breakfast — crisp bacon, buttery biscuits, and eggs — hung in the air like a familiar, comforting song.

Marion Franklin stood by the table, her hands deft and practiced as she adjusted a plate with the rhythm of long repetition. The subtle scent of butter and flour clung faintly to her dress — a quiet badge of her industrious morning. Her movements were steady, purposeful, an unspoken ceremony of love woven into the day's first meal.

In one corner of the room, a tall bookcase stood like a silent guardian. Its shelves were lined with a carefully curated collection: novels with cracked, dog-eared spines; well-thumbed volumes of classic plays; and thick academic tomes gilded with gold lettering that caught the slanting sunlight and shimmered softly. These books were more than mere objects — they were the quiet testimony of a woman who valued education as both vocation and passion. Marion had poured her life into learning, and then teaching, and these companions lined her walls as a testament to that enduring devotion.

From the bedroom, through the open door, Jack Franklin's voice drifted out — warm, mellow, still brushed with sleep.

"That's wonderful! Thank you, Marion."

She smiled faintly at the sound, a small softening around her eyes. Straightening her back, she pulled out a chair and settled into it with quiet grace. Her hands folded gently in her lap as she closed her eyes for a brief moment — a silent breath, a pause of gratitude and steadiness before the day unfurled fully.

From deeper in the apartment, familiar footsteps echoed softly over the wooden floor.

The swish and tug of fabric, the careful rearranging of clothing, marked Jack's slow awakening.

"Say," he called, his voice warmer now, steadier, "I meant to ask how your latest project is coming along. Your students must be runnin' around in circles tryin' to learn their lines."

Marion opened her eyes, a quiet laugh bubbling up from deep within, a faint smile tugging at the corners of her lips as she reached for her napkin, folding it with gentle care in her lap.

"Oh, they certainly are," she replied, calm and amused. "We're preparing to perform Doctor Faustus by Christopher Marlowe for the university's constituents."

From the doorway, Jack appeared, half-dressed, one leg awkwardly raised as he wrestled into his trousers. His brow lifted in a mix of curiosity and mild bewilderment.

"Doctor Faustus?" he echoed, tilting his head with playful disbelief.

"Yes," Marion said, her voice soft, just tinged with amusement at his reaction. "You'd think a 16th-century Elizabethan text would be difficult for them to grasp, but surprisingly, it isn't. They're genuinely excited about it."

Jack plopped down at the edge of the bed, his shoulders hunched in that familiar slump of early morning fatigue. He leaned forward, fingers moving quickly and expertly as they threaded through the worn leather of his shoelaces. "It certainly would be difficult for me," he muttered under his breath, voice thick with sleep. "Why not give them something less complicated?"

Marion shrugged gently, her face serene, untroubled by his protest. "Because I have high expectations for them. And like I said — they've taken to it very well."

Jack pushed off the bed and stood, now fully dressed, his suspenders taut over the broad planes of his shoulders, and his shirt crisp and neatly pressed — the result of Marion's meticulous care the night before. He crossed to her side, leaning down to press a soft kiss on her cheek. It was a simple gesture, but heavy with unspoken gratitude and affection.

Marion closed her eyes for a heartbeat, savoring the moment. Her heart swelled, warmed not only by the kiss itself but by everything it represented. Jack wasn't just her husband—he was her partner, her steadfast ally in a world that often sought to wear people down. She thought, briefly, of the women she knew: women with tired eyes and sharp tempers, who lived in silence beneath the weight of harsher realities. She was one of the lucky ones.

Jack settled into his chair at the table, his appetite now fully awakened. He began filling his plate with eggs and bacon, the savory aroma making his mouth water. He took a bite, chewing slowly and appreciatively, but his gaze flicked to the wall clock. His eyes widened as he caught the time, nearly choking on the morsel.

"Oh, I better run," he said hurriedly, wiping his hands on the napkin with a sudden urgency. "Harold and the rest of the boys will be outside the shop soon."

With a smooth motion, he stood, leaving half his plate untouched. He reached for his coat, draped over the back of a chair, sliding his arms into it with practiced speed. Another kiss landed on Marion's cheek, gentle but quick, as he prepared to step out.

"By the way," Marion said, voice deliberately casual but threaded with quiet anticipation, "we received a correspondence from the Browns the other day."

Jack's hand paused on the doorknob. He turned slightly, eyebrows lifting. "Really? How surprising."

Marion lifted her teacup, sipping with composed grace. "Well, they are friends of ours, after all. They're having a celebration for Abigail tonight. She's engaged, you know. I wrote back and told them we would come. The note's over there, if you'd like to read it."

A flicker of something—unease, perhaps—crossed Jack's face, subtle but unmistakable in the crease of his brow. "I can't believe the Browns are having anything with all the turmoil going on in the city the other night. Don't they know what happened?"

Yes, last night another woman was found dead. Her throat had been slashed. The papers called the alleged perpetrator by one name and one name alone - the Atlanta Ripper.

The city had been shaken to the core ever since the deaths began. The fashions in which the victims were killed were the same. Always a slit throat…always a woman…always a Black woman.

Marion set the cup down with a delicate clink, eyes steady. "I'm sure they do. I can't make heads or tails of it either — especially since it was all over the papers. I'd wager the whole city is worried."

Jack glanced toward the small side table where the note lay folded neatly beside the morning's newspaper. He was tempted to reach for it, but the relentless ticking of the clock pulled his attention back.

"I'll look at it later," he said finally.

"Don't forget to come home early so we can dress for the party tonight," she reminded him softly but clearly.

"Alright," Jack nodded. "See you this evening, Marion."

The door closed behind him with a soft click, sealing Marion once again within the calm of the apartment.

She sat still for a long moment, eyes lingering on the breakfast table now disrupted — plates half-full, crumbs scattered, a momentary chaos amid the morning's quiet.

Her fingers traced the edge of her plate lightly, and a soft sigh escaped her lips, barely audible in the hush that returned.

There would be cleaning now — dishes to be washed, food to be wrapped and stored in the icebox. With practiced motions and a heart already drifting elsewhere, she rose and began to gather the plates. Her thoughts had shifted, no longer on the Browns, or the city's turmoil, but on the young voices soon to echo in rehearsal.

CHAPTER 3

JACK

T he sun bore down on Atlanta with the weight of a furnace, unforgiving and absolute. As Jack Franklin stepped out from the modest shadow of the apartment building, the heat wrapped around him like a second skin—wet, heavy, and inescapably alive. The moment his soles hit the sidewalk, the city's breath engulfed him: a mingled perfume of scorched dust, tobacco smoke curling from early-morning pipes, and the tang of fried batter wafting from curbside vendors already hard at work. The humidity rose off the streets in slow waves, shimmering like some ghostly tide trying to lift itself free of the stone.

He paused just outside the threshold, adjusting the collar of his freshly pressed shirt. Already, the cotton clung stubbornly to the nape of his neck, wilting beneath the sun's persistent attention. Behind him, the red brick of the apartment building radiated yesterday's heat, as though it had never truly cooled. Before him, Atlanta was already in motion.

The city moved like a restless beast. Its arteries throbbed with commerce and conversation. Vendors barked their wares from curbside stands—boiled peanuts, iced Coca-Cola, cigars fresh from Havana—while the iron-rimmed wheels of wagons rattled over cobblestones slick with morning dew and the sweat of beasts. A church bell rang faintly in the distance, but closer, sharper, came the mechanical clang of the streetcar bell—metal striking metal in clear, punctual warning. It rang with the finality of law, of routine. It rang like Atlanta's heartbeat.

At the far end of the block, the electric streetcar shuddered to a halt, its roof hissing with steam, as though the machine itself resented the heat. Jack walked toward it at a steady pace. There was no reason to rush—he had learned long ago that time in this city wasn't a straight line, but a cycle, a loop, spinning with the wheels of trolleys and the rhythm of labor. It would come around again.

He boarded with ease, the wooden floor giving a tired groan beneath his step. Inside, the air was even thicker, saturated with the musk of leather seats, the coppery scent of oil and smoke, and the human tang of men already baking in their coats and ties. Above the aisle, affixed like scripture, a sign declared in stark black letters: "COLORED ONLY." The typeface was clean. Unapologetic. Not loud, but louder than it needed to be.

Jack's eyes barely lingered on it. His feet carried him past rows of white passengers whose gazes drifted toward him and away again, not with curiosity, nor contempt, but with something colder—indifference calcified into habit. He slipped into the rear section, settling beside an older Black man. The man gave Jack a brief nod— neither friendly nor cold, but something in between. A nod of shared understanding. That was enough.

The streetcar lurched forward with a sighing whine. The city began to scroll past the windows — shopfronts flickering by like pages of a story he already knew too well. Inside the carriage, soft voices rose and fell, exchanging gossip, plans, and prayers. Outside, Atlanta roared on. Jack leaned back, his hands resting on his knees, his eyes trained on the horizon beyond the glass.

The ride was long. Not in miles, but in what it demanded you carry with you — heat, silence, the invisible weight of lines drawn not on streets, but in minds. Yet he sat with the calm of a man who had learned long ago that dignity, when not given, could still be kept.

Outside, Atlanta stretched itself wide, like a stage summoned into being just for morning's performance. The streets brimmed with color and noise — striped awnings casting scalloped shadows over storefronts, baskets of fruit and bolts of cloth spilling onto the sidewalks, their hues bright against the smudged haze of urban dust. Children tore through the spaces between stoops and stoic lampposts, their bare feet slapping against sun-warmed stone, their laughter rising sharp and weightless above the deeper hum of the city's grind. Newsboys barked their headlines into the air, voices cracked and hoarse from repetition: fragments of violence, politics, unrest—each word skimming across the day like a thrown stone.

As the streetcar turned eastward, the tone of the landscape shifted. Downtown's pale facades and symmetrical avenues gave way to Sweet Auburn—a district with its own heartbeat. Auburn Avenue, or "Sweet Auburn" as it was lovingly referred to, was the center of Black business in Atlanta, and Jack's shop was one of its most coveted landmarks. The streets here didn't just breathe; they spoke. Hand-painted signs adorned the buildings like badges of survival and pride—announcing the presence of tailors, midwives, pastors, lawyers, and confectioners. Wooden stoops gave way to polished doorframes, and narrow windows framed busy interiors filled with talk, music, and motion. Sweet Auburn didn't wait to be seen. It stood. It declared.

People walked taller here. Their steps were rooted, their postures erect—not in arrogance, but in claim. This was earned ground. A haven carved not from charity, but from grit, perseverance, and communal will. Every storefront was a statement: We are here. We are building. We are not going anywhere.

At the heart of this proud artery stood Jack's barbershop. The wooden sign above its door, "Jack's Barber Shop," bore lettering in gold leaf that time had softened, but not erased. The curves and serifs still gleamed faintly in the sunlight, weathered yet defiant. Out front, a small crowd had already begun to gather, congregating in pockets of shade where they shifted their weight from foot to foot and dabbed glistening brows with faded kerchiefs. Some were his barbers, aprons folded beneath their arms; others were loyal customers who knew this place as much for its camaraderie as its clippers.

Inside the streetcar, Jack leaned slightly to glance out the window. The vehicle hissed and groaned, easing toward its stop. Beside him, a man in suspenders and a wide, sun-bleached hat leaned forward for a better view.

"Well now," the man drawled, squinting past the pane. "Looks like you got your work cut out for you today, Jack."

Jack didn't turn. He simply smiled, a quiet exhale escaping his nose.

"I suppose I do."

He stood, the weight of the day already collecting in the hollows of his shoulders. As he stepped off the streetcar, the heat met him like a returning companion— familiar, pressing, absolute. The soles of his shoes kissed the sidewalk with resolve, and almost instantly, the knot of men outside the shop turned in unison, as though gravity had shifted in his direction.

"Morning, boys!" he called, raising his voice just enough to lift above the hum of the neighborhood. A smile curved across his face, unhurried and easy. "Glad to see everybody's still got their teeth and tempers intact."

From within the cluster, Charlie Howard stepped forward, already mid-performance. Stout, brash, and eternally loud, Charlie had the showmanship of a preacher and the timing of a vaudevillian.

"Don't give us that smooth talk, Jack!" he shouted, fanning himself with a rolled-up newspaper. "You know how long we been waitin' out here? Man, we cookin' like bacon on a griddle!"

Jack was already reaching into his pocket, fishing for the shop key. He raised a brow without looking up.

"No, I don't, Charlie. But I've got a feelin' you're fixin' to tell me."

"Thirty minutes!" Charlie thundered, slapping a hand to his chest like a wounded witness. "Some of these poor fellas been out here even longer. We done baked, broiled, and blackened."

Jack chuckled under his breath, sliding the key into the lock with a practiced flick.

"Don't listen to him, Mr. Franklin," Bill Johnson said, stepping forward with the polished decorum of a man who ironed his bowler hat. "Ain't even been ten minutes."

"Yeah," Lou Granger added, pushing his glasses up the bridge of his nose with one amused finger. "Charlie's just tryin' to put on a show."

Charlie spun around with a look of theatrical offense, arms flung wide like he'd just been accused in court.

"I can't trust none of you!" he bellowed, but the grin betrayed him. Around him, the others laughed — shoulders relaxing, voices rising, the tension of waiting giving way to the familiar ease of ritual.

"Sure can't!" Abraham Williamson laughed, his voice rich with the lilting cadence of the islands, warm and easy as a breeze over saltwater. "We'll give you away every time."

The bell above the door let out its cheerful jingle as Jack eased it open, ushering in the scent that had become synonymous with memory itself—pomade, cedar, shaving cream, and the faintest whisper of bay rum clinging to the walls like an old story told often. Sunlight lanced through the wide front windows, illuminating the row of barber chairs that stood in a solemn line, like seasoned soldiers waiting quietly for orders.

Jack held the door open, and the men followed, their laughter lingering in the doorway like a final note from a brass horn. Inside, the shop seemed to exhale—stretching awake, shaking off sleep.

The morning unfurled gently, like the slow turning of a well-worn page. As the door clicked shut behind them, the rhythm of the shop took hold—measured, habitual, rooted in repetition and the kind of dignity that didn't have to be announced. Men filtered in gradually, in no rush, each step deliberate. They came not as customers but as keepers of tradition, nodding their greetings with brief eye contact, a tug of the brim, a wordless understanding that here, in this space, life was allowed to slow.

No one needed to fill the silence — it was already full. Familiar creaks of aged floorboards. The soft scrape of chairs against tile. The occasional ahem as someone cleared their throat. Words were secondary in such places; what mattered was presence.

Jack crossed to the front windows, his movement steady, unrushed. With two pulls, he lifted the shades, allowing the morning to spill in unfiltered. Light poured across the black-and-white tiled floor, scattering long amber streaks like offerings. Dust floated in slow motion, catching the sun's golden fingers and turning lazy circles through the warmth.

The shop was small, yes — but it held time. Not just hours, but decades. Its walls bore the weight of unspoken stories and small kindnesses, the laughter of boys turned men and men turned gray. This place had not been built, it had become — grown into its skin through wear and memory.

The barber chairs, lined up against the mirrored wall, each bore their own particular history. One leaned just a hair to the left, its spine never quite straight. Another let out a low groan every time its footrest was dropped. The third had a scar across the arm — no one could recall the moment it appeared, only that it had always been there. They weren't flaws; they were fingerprints.

Above them, the wide mirrors reflected the weary but expectant faces of the morning crowd — men ready to be shaped back into themselves. The kind of grooming that went deeper than the skin. The act of becoming presentable again. Respectable. Fresh.

Behind the chairs, the shelves stood neat and prepared. Rows of glass bottles and metal tins stood like altar offerings — aftershaves that bit the skin and woke the senses, stiff-bristled brushes aligned just so, blades polished to gleam under the light. The scent of antiseptic clung faintly in the background, tempered by the sweeter, spicier notes of sandalwood and clove, creating a scent that was unmistakably, unchangeably Jack's.

Jack moved through the space like a man reading a book he'd written. His hands knew the drawers by memory; his fingers found the tools without looking. The towel steamer hissed softly as he filled it with fresh water.

Brushes were unfurled, clippers arranged in lines. It was a ritual, but it was never rushed. There was reverence in it.

No one interrupted. No one needed to.

The shop was speaking now. It spoke in rhythms — the soft clap of towels, the creak of leather, the murmur of baritones caught mid-thought. It spoke in the way men sat back and allowed themselves to be taken care of, even just for a moment.

Then came Charlie — predictably, inevitably — the first to pierce the quiet with his usual mischief. He twisted in his chair, elbows hooked lazily over the armrests, turning just enough to catch Jack in his line of sight. There it was — that glint in his eye, equal parts trouble and charm, and the crooked smile that always seemed on the verge of a joke.

"You know I had to get in at least one crack before the morning really started, didn't you, Jack?"

Jack didn't flinch, didn't even pause. Still working the final blind into place, he let out a soft chuckle, the sound low and familiar — like a screen door swinging shut behind a friend.

"I sure did, Charlie," he replied, not turning to look. "Been wonderin' how long it'd take you today. Might be a new record."

Charlie puffed out his chest, lifting his chin like a man being knighted for services in sarcasm. He stood as if accepting an imaginary medal — shoulders squared, expression mock-solemn.

"Well then," he said, the grin now full and unabashed, "put my name in the paper."

Their laughter rose together — easy, unforced, and weathered by time. It wasn't the kind of laugh reserved for punchlines or clever timing. It was the laughter of men who had seen each other through marriages and funerals, slow seasons and storm warnings. The kind that softened grief, sanded the edges of long weeks, and stitched together the mornings with a thread stronger than words.

Charlie slid back into his usual spot, one hip cocked comfortably against the worn arm of his favored chair, just as the front door creaked open again with a sigh of hinges and a rush of warm air.

A man stepped inside, the sort whose face had been weathered by wind and time, but whose eyes still carried something sharp and knowing. He gave Jack a subtle nod — one of those gestures that said everything and nothing. To Charlie, he offered a wink, the kind shared only by men who had swapped stories over clinking glasses or Saturday fishing lines.

He found his seat near the fan, settling in with the ease of someone who'd been doing this for years.

Now that the shop was open for the morning, Charlie set up behind his usual place at his chair. A customer sat down in front of him.

Jack settled at his own station. He already had a customer, so he started working. He knew more customers would soon be coming.

"You heard about Lena Sharp?" asked one of the customers.

The joyous atmosphere and smiles died instantly.

Jack tried reining in the discussion.

"We all heard."

"I heard this morning," the customer continued. "Sad what happened to her. It truly is."

"Don't the law got a lead yet?" Abraham asked.

"Those upstanding White policemen?" Charlie snorted with a sarcastic tone. "I think they're too busy doing other things!"

There were some snickers and rolls of the eyes. The joke was a bit heavy-handed, but it was not lost on Jack.

Jack knew that a lot of White people in the South falsely viewed African Americans as wild and unpredictable – to be feared like a boogeyman under the bed.

It was highly unlikely that the police here in the Jim Crow South would work hard to find this killer. The victims had all been Black women.

Nonetheless, something had to be done to stop the murders, and soon.

Jack wished he could do something, but he couldn't. He felt helpless, but he remembered that he and the other men in the shop had to be brave – for themselves and the people they loved.

Things were so uncertain now, but each of the men knew they had to do their best to live. The very act of living was an act of bravery. They had to fight the good fight one hour at a time, one day at a time.

As he continued to work, Jack said a silent prayer in his head for Lena Sharp and her daughter Emma Lou, who was almost killed by the Ripper as well but survived. He hoped for the best.

The hum of clippers broke the silence next — a single click, clear and certain, like the downbeat of a song everyone already knew. The sound filled the shop like the opening note of a well-rehearsed symphony, rising to meet the faint rhythm of ceiling fans and the low murmur of men in mid-conversation.

Jack moved behind his customer without announcement. A crisp white cape snapped in the air and fluttered down over broad shoulders, settling like a curtain before a performance. His hands moved with the grace of someone whose artistry lay not in flash, but in repetition — in knowing exactly when to turn the head, where to press the comb, how to guide the clippers like a painter working from muscle memory.

49

Each motion was confident, clean. The kind of quiet precision earned not through training but through living — through knowing that a good cut wasn't just about style, but trust. And Jack had long since earned theirs.

The shop swelled gently with movement. A boot scraped across tile. Laughter murmured low. Outside, the world marched on, fast and hungry. But in here, time shaped itself to a different pace — slower, deeper, truer.

CHAPTER 4

MARION

Elsewhere in the city, far from the barbershop's easy banter and hum of clippers, the late morning sun streamed through the tall windows of a classroom at Atlanta University. It spilled across rows of scarred wooden desks, polishing them with gold and shadow. Years of restless hands, hurried scribbles, and whispered ambition had worn the surfaces smooth, and now the sunlight painted them like altars of thought. Dust motes drifted in the beams like quiet echoes — memories suspended in light, the residue of a thousand lectures and silent revelations.

The air was thick with the scent of chalk and old paper, and something heavier still: the weight of knowledge. Knowledge hard-won, passed down, fought for. The blackboards bore faint traces of past lessons, their surfaces ghosted with chalk lines that refused to fade—like the memories of thinkers who had come before.

At the front of the room stood Professor Marion Franklin.

She did not need to raise her voice to hold the room. She never had. Her poise alone—shoulders squared, spine unyielding, gaze unhurried—carried authority. Not the kind that demanded attention, but the kind that made you want to give it. She wore a sharply tailored dress of deep navy that drew out the rich warmth of her skin, and her hair was pinned in place with the kind of precision that told you nothing in her life was left untended. There was pride in her bearing—not arrogance, but earned dignity, passed down through generations and shaped by struggle.

Her eyes swept the classroom. Nearly twenty African American students sat in neat rows, some scribbling quietly, others with pens stilled midair — each caught in varying degrees of anticipation and hesitation.

Behind Marion, the blackboard bore today's theme in clean, assertive strokes of chalk:

Doctor Faustus – Emotion and Damnation She turned to face them fully, her hand resting lightly on the edge of the desk.

"Now," she said, her voice calm and honey-rich, with the deliberate cadence of someone who expected to be listened to and usually was, "who here can inform me how a player in a stage performance evokes emotion from an audience?"

The question hung in the air, unhurried.

A hush fell, not of discomfort but of thought. Pens paused. Eyes shifted — some downward, others sideways, the universal choreography of students hoping someone else might take the leap first.

Marion let the silence stretch, but not out of cruelty. She understood its value. Silence could be a teacher, too — a space where thoughts formed, deepened, and clarified.

"No one?" she asked gently, a note of encouragement softening the edges of her tone.

"Alright, then let's narrow the field. Consider evocation as it relates to the character of Dr. Faustus."

Still no hands.

Until—finally—a slender arm rose from the third row, hesitant but brave.

Marion's face lit with quiet approval. "Yes, Margaret?"

The girl shifted in her seat, voice small but sincere. "Well... at the end of the play... Faustus regrets what he's done. He has second thoughts."

"Very good," Marion nodded, stepping slightly forward. "But how is that shown? What tools does the actor use? How does the audience know he feels remorse?"

A pause again, and then, near the window, another hand lifted—this one less tentative. Joseph, tall and soft- spoken, flipped open his worn copy of the text, pages fluttering like a book well-loved and often leaned on. He found the passage and read aloud, his voice gathering strength with each line:

"'Cursed be the parents that engendered me: No, Faustus, curse thy self, curse Lucifer, That hath deprived thee of the joys of heaven.'"

Marion's smile deepened — not broad, but meaningful. "Exactly. Through his words. Through the unraveling of his speech. The actor must not simply recite — he must bleed. We must feel the fear, the grief, the desperation pouring from him. Faustus realizes — far too late — what he's lost. His doom is no longer looming; it's arrived."

She stepped out from behind the desk now, her voice quieting as it grew more profound.

"And what lesson, class, can we gather from this tale?"

Another pause. Then, from the back, Philip — broad-shouldered and often skeptical — raised his hand with a half-grin. "Never get involved in shady dealings?"

The room broke into soft laughter — muffled, but genuine.

Marion allowed herself a brief smile. "It's humorous," she said, "but not untrue. Still, I think the truth we seek lies deeper."

She walked slowly to her desk and picked up the leather-bound Bible that lay atop a stack of papers, the binding worn but reverently kept. With both hands, she carried it across the room and extended it to Philip.

"Turn, please, to Mark chapter eight, verse thirty-six."

Philip took the Bible, his fingers gingerly parting the thin pages, and read aloud:

"For what shall it profit a man, if he shall gain the whole world, and lose his own soul?"

A hush fell again, but this time it was different— heavier. The room was no longer just a place of lectures. It was now a chamber of reflection.

Marion gave a single, solemn nod. "Very good."

And then it came—the sound that always made the walls seem older, the day seem longer. From somewhere high above the university's stone spires, the deep chimes of the old bell tower rang out, one after another, slow and deliberate, reverberating through the glass panes and settling like a hush upon the classroom. It was noon, and outside, the world moved forward as if nothing had changed.

"That's all for today," Marion said, rising from her chair with a practiced cadence, her voice composed but commanding. "Remember, your lines must be memorized by Monday. No exceptions. A play is not a reading—it's a reckoning."

There was a faint rustling as the students stirred. Chairs scraped gently against the floor, a low murmur of parting words filled the room like soft smoke, and backpacks were slung over shoulders with the weary familiarity of routine. The mood lifted palpably—as if the bell had rung not just for the hour but to grant them release from responsibility. Outside, there would be sun, chatter, perhaps a late lunch with friends.

But not for Margaret.

She hadn't moved. Still seated in the third row, hands folded tightly in her lap, her gaze pinned to a fixed point on the desk in front of her. The others didn't notice—too busy gathering their belongings and their afternoon plans—but Marion did. She always did.

She stepped closer, her heels soundless against the polished floor, her voice softened with instinctive care. "Margaret? Is something the matter?"

The young woman looked up only slightly, her posture still withdrawn, chin angled down as though retreating into herself. "Nothing too much, Professor Franklin. It's just…" The words trailed off as she fumbled with her fingers, twisting them over and over in her lap like she might wring the truth from them.

Marion didn't press, not immediately. Instead, she eased herself onto the edge of the desk beside her, reducing the height between them, her presence a quiet offering of reassurance rather than authority. "It's alright," she said gently. "You can tell me."

Margaret lifted her eyes then, and the moment they met Marion's, the wall she'd been trying so hard to keep intact gave way. Her gaze shimmered, glassy and uncertain. "I'm just scared," she whispered, her voice so thin it barely reached across the space between them.

Marion drew in a slow breath, her chest tightening. She didn't need Margaret to elaborate. She already knew. Everyone did, though they said little and speculated more. Emma Lou's name had been on every tongue that week, passed like a secret and spoken like a prayer. And her mother — God help her — was no longer just a woman. She had become a headline.

"I see," Marion said, her voice hushed, tinged with sorrow. And she did. She saw all of it — the fear that bloomed in the shadow of violence, the grief that came too early, too sharp, too real for someone Margaret's age.

"She and I..." Margaret began again, voice trembling, "we were the same age. Grew up just a few streets apart. Played together when we were little." She paused, swiped a hand across one cheek though the tear had already fallen. "Then one day... her mama's gone.

Just like that. She's dead. And now it's everywhere. The papers, the radio, everyone talking about it like she's a story and not a person."

There was a brittle edge to her voice, a mix of fear and quiet rage that cracked through the sorrow.

Marion reached out then, laying a warm, steady hand on her shoulder. "I know, darling. I know." She tried to keep her tone even, calm, but there was a tremor at the edges—an unspoken grief of her own that she hadn't yet dared give shape. "They'll find him," she said, though even to her own ears, the words rang like a promise she wasn't entirely sure she could keep. "They'll catch whoever did this. I'm certain."

But Margaret only shook her head, and when she spoke again, her voice was barely more than breath. "Emma Lou got away from him... but what if I'm next?"

And there it was—the real terror, not just of the thing that had happened, but the thing that might still.

Marion's jaw tightened, her expression sharpening— not in anger, but in something older and deeper. A fierce protectiveness rose in her, maternal and immediate. She lowered herself until she was kneeling, so their eyes were level. Her voice was different now—no longer soft, but firm, clear, unwavering.

"No," she said. "You mustn't talk like that. Do you hear me? Don't let fear speak louder than your sense. You are smart, Margaret. And you are strong. You keep your eyes open. You stay cautious, and you trust your instincts. But don't let him take your spirit, too. Don't give him that."

She reached into the pocket of her cardigan and pulled out a soft handkerchief, pressing it gently to Margaret's cheek. Her hands were steady, deliberate. The kind of hands that had held others together many times before.

"Keep your head up. Walk with care, yes — but walk with purpose. That's how we survive. That's how we win."

Margaret stared at her, searching. And in Marion's eyes, she found what she needed — something unshakable, forged not in certainty but in will. She nodded slowly, her shoulders relaxing just enough to breathe again. "Thank you, Professor," she said, her voice steadier, with a quiet steel threaded through it now.

"You're welcome, dear," Marion replied, rising to her feet.

Margaret stood, adjusted her bag, and offered a faint, grateful smile before turning toward the door. She didn't look back. And when the door clicked shut behind her, the room exhaled into silence once more.

Outside, the sunlight slanted across the university green, but its warmth no longer reached the floor where Marion stood. She moved toward the window and clasped her hands in front of her, gazing out as students strolled across the lawn — laughing, talking, their lives continuing with the innocence of those who still believed themselves untouched by darkness.

But Marion knew better. She watched them, her eyes distant.

Something had shifted. Not just in Margaret. Not just in their quiet community. But in the world itself — something subtle yet seismic, a fault line now running just beneath the surface.

And for the first time in a very long while, Marion Franklin felt the full, unrelenting weight of that shift settle deep in her chest.

Later that evening, it was a warm summer night. The excitement of the 4th of July could be felt in the demeanors of the citizens of Atlanta throughout the day.

Though, considering the unfortunate events that recently plagued the city, the festivities were slightly subdued.

Many families and their close friends had traded the Independence Day bashes that usually took place outside for quiet, more contained celebrations inside their homes.

Inside Jack and Marion's comfortable apartment, both Marion and Jack were getting dressed for the celebration that would take place at the Brown's residence later that night. Jack was tying his tie and adjusting his black suit. Marion sat at her mirror, slipping on one of her bracelets and putting the finishing touches to the elegant deep green night dress she was wearing.

"Honey, you won't believe what happened at the shop today," said Jack. "That Charlie is such a kidder. He was talkin' about this new gal he's seeing. He…"

Jack stopped mid-sentence. He realized his wife wasn't listening.

He walked over to her, concerned. "Everything alright, dear?"

Marion looked up at the reflection of Jack's face in the mirror as he stood behind her.

"What? Oh, yes," Marion replied.

Jack gave her a skeptical look. He knew there was something more.

Marion opened her lips as if to say something but closed them with a neat smile as if to appear that she forgot what she was about to say.

She looked away briefly before finally giving in, "Alright. During class today, one of the students confided in me how frightened she was about everything that's been happening."

Jack gave an understanding nod.

"She's not the only one," he began. "That's all the boys could talk about in the shop today. Did you know Harold goes to the same church Lena Sharp went to?"

"Just about the whole town is in a panic," added Marion. "I'm surprised Winston and Mabel are even having this party for Abigail. Do you still think we should go?"

"Of course. You already told them we'd be there."

Marion raised her arms in dismay.

"You're right. Will you help me with this?"

She was holding a necklace in place around her neck.

Jack walked over to fasten it.

"Maybe they wanted to carry on in the hopes everyone would forget about what's happening?" Jack suggested.

As he fastened the necklace, his fingers grazed the side of her neck. Her soft skin sent jolts of delight throughout his body.

Jack was so happy to have Marion as his wife. He never had been happier in his life than when he was with Marion. She was an angel of beauty that glowed with a captivating serenity and he was inspired by her perseverance.

Jack caught his breath as he looked at Marion's smooth neck.

He almost dared to kiss it.

He controlled his desire and stepped back after the necklace had finally been fastened.

"Thank you," Marion replied. "Sure."

They both headed towards the door. Jack could no longer contain it. He grabbed Marion by the hips and stopped her in place.

"Who says we have to be on time?" he asked. He looked adoringly into her eyes.

Marion was both surprised and flattered. Jack caressed her cheek and began to kiss her.

She gave him a coy smile. "Oh, Jack. You know how much I despise being late."

"Just a few minutes?"

There was a brief pause between them.

"Do you remember what happened last time?"

Marion asked somberly.

Jack paused.

"What if it happens again?"

Marion's face was serious. Jack knew just what she was talking about. He was hoping she wouldn't bring it up, but he guessed there was no time like the present. Instead of giving into her doubts, Jack attempted to reassure her.

"Who knows? This may be our chance," Jack said with an optimistic tone.

Marion rolled her eyes. "I can't go through that again, Jack. I just can't."

She paused. She looked into Jack's eyes. Jack took her hand in his and kissed it.

"Marion," said Jack. "I was disappointed too. Hearing that baby call us 'ma' and 'pa' and watching it grow was all I ever wanted - just like you did."

He held her face in his palms. Her eyes were filled with tears. "I'm here for you. Maybe this time will be different. Can we at least try?"

She hesitated, staring at him with a slight gaze. She wiped the tears from her eyes.

"I'm not a young woman anymore, Jack," she said. "Perhaps it's just not for us."

Marion slowly pulled away from him. She headed towards the bedroom door and said grievously, "We ought to get going. We don't want to be late."

Jack was disappointed. After she had left the bedroom, he knew there was nothing more he could say that would make Marion change her mind towards the subject of possibly starting a family. Their dream of being parents had been defeated, but he wasn't giving up – not on Marion or their dream of nurturing a child.

Before long, Jack took a deep breath and mentally prepared himself for the evening ahead. Having fully gathered himself, he soon followed Marion out of the apartment.

The faint clatter of hooves against cobblestone echoed down the dusky lane, slow and deliberate, as the carriage came to a graceful stop before the Browns' stately home. Twilight had not yet yielded to night; the sky above was brushed with lingering streaks of rose and indigo, while golden lanterns lining the walkway flickered to life one by one, casting pools of amber light that danced across the brick path.

Jack was the first to descend, stepping lightly onto the gravel before turning to offer his hand to Marion. She placed her gloved fingers in his with the ease of long companionship, and the soft rustle of her evening dress barely rose above the gentle creak of the carriage springs. The driver, silent but watchful, tipped his hat in acknowledgment as Jack handed over the fare. Without a word, the man flicked the reins, and the horse ambled forward once more, wheels creaking into the growing quiet.

They stood for a moment in the stillness, gazing up at the home before them. The Browns' residence loomed not with menace, but with the imposing dignity of age and wealth — an elegant and spacious Classical Revival two-story home with Beaux Arts influences sat at the end of a path. The estate had tall white columns and an immaculate facade, touched now with the softened blush of dusk as it sat at the end of a short path. Marion looked at the house, gleefully impressed. Gaslight spilled warmly from the tall windows, casting soft silhouettes of movement and revelry inside.

Marion exhaled, her breath curling faintly in the cool air. "Beautiful as always," she murmured, eyes tracing the elegant cornices and arching windows with silent admiration.

Jack smiled, taking her hand once more. "It's definitely something," he said, though his tone was more cautious — less in awe, more in anticipation.

The gravel crunched softly beneath their steps as they approached the front porch, where laughter and music were already pulsing behind thick oak walls. Marion straightened the collar of her dress, instinctively smoothing a strand of hair behind her ear.

"Sounds lively," she said, glancing sideways at him.

"It always is here," Jack replied. "Especially when Abigail's involved."

He reached out and pressed the brass doorbell. A gentle chime rang through the wood, and for a moment they were suspended in the hush that follows arrival — the breath between expectation and embrace.

The door opened with a soft creak. Framed in the light stood Winston Brown — African American, tall, and composed, his eyes crinkling at the corners with the warmth of recognition. His spectacles glinted in the gaslight as he broke into a broad grin.

"Well, if it isn't the Franklins!" he boomed, stepping forward like a man welcoming kin, not guests.

Marion offered her hand, which Winston took with gentlemanly charm. "Winston," she said, her smile polite, measured. "Still the grand host, I see."

Jack followed with a firm handshake. "Good to see you, friend."

"Oh, come now," Winston chuckled, stepping back with a sweep of his arm. "Don't just stand out there and catch your deaths. Get in here!"

The foyer embraced them with immediate warmth— physically and emotionally. The scent of roast meat and sweet spices curled in the air, laced with the more delicate fragrances of lavender and orange blossom from the floral arrangements that flanked the stairway.

Everything gleamed—mahogany floors buffed to a mirror shine, high ceilings etched with ornate crown molding, the chandeliers above twinkling like constellations fallen to earth.

Winston took their coats and hung them gently on the polished brass rack, murmuring some pleasantry about the number of guests who'd already arrived. Marion's eyes followed the coats for a moment longer than necessary, then drifted back to the hallway ahead—where music, clinking glasses, and laughter floated from the parlor like moths to flame.

"Right this way," Winston said, already leading them toward the glow.

71

Jack offered Marion his arm again, and she took it— though her fingers tightened slightly as they walked. There was warmth in the air. Comfort. Celebration. But somewhere in the distance, beneath the music and laughter, the night seemed to whisper of something else. Something that waited.

CHAPTER 5

JACK

The parlor was a vision of elegance, with its Rococo embellishments curling along the moldings like ivory vines. A soft golden glow filled the room, catching on the velvet upholstery and the glossy sheen of the grand piano nestled in the far corner. Plush chairs and sofas framed a small, ornate table in the center, and although Jack and Marion had expected a bustling crowd, the space was filled with only a modest gathering—perhaps ten guests, all of them African American except a kind-looking, white reverend who was also present. Most of the people in the room were couples, chatting softly over drinks or seated in gentle clusters around the room.

Against one wall sat an unlit fireplace, flanked by marble busts and floral arrangements, and near it stood the unmistakable silhouette of the Brown family — gracious as ever, regal without arrogance.

Mabel Brown, radiant in a sea-blue gown that matched the sparkle in her eyes, looked up from her conversation on the sofa and beamed. "Jack! Marion! Wonderful to see you," she said warmly, crossing the room with open arms. She embraced them both in turn, her perfume floral and familiar.

"Hello, Mabel," Jack said with a fond smile.

"So nice seeing you again," Marion added, holding Mabel's hands a moment longer.

"Thank you both for coming. I was so glad when you wrote that you would come," Mabel said, stepping back with visible delight.

"Oh, we wouldn't miss this for the world," Marion replied.

Jack's gaze wandered across the room and returned to Mabel. "Where is Abigail? Let's meet the young man who's stolen her heart."

At this, Mabel's expression brightened further. She turned and gestured to the other side of the room, where a young couple stood by the fireplace, exchanging quiet words. "Come," she said, leading them.

The couple turned as they approached. Abigail, now in her early twenties, carried the same elegant composure as her mother but with the softness of youth. Her dark hair was pulled back in soft waves, and the blush in her cheeks deepened when she saw Jack and Marion.

"Jack, Marion, you remember Abigail?" Mabel asked with a hand gently placed on her daughter's shoulder.

"Congratulations!" Jack said at once.

"So proud of you, dear," Marion added with genuine warmth.

"Thank you!" Abigail smiled, her joy bubbling just beneath her calm demeanor.

"And this," Mabel continued, placing a hand on the young man's arm, "is her fiancé, Uriah Oliver."

Uriah stepped forward with a polite nod, a trace of self-consciousness behind his confident smile. His hair was neatly parted, and his suit was well-fitted but not overly flashy. He gave off the impression of someone still adjusting to the spotlight.

"Uriah's a fine young man," Winston interjected, arriving at Mabel's side with a nod of approval.

"He certainly is," Mabel echoed.

Uriah gave a bashful laugh. "Well, thank you, Mr. and Mrs. Brown. I'm so lucky to have met Abigail. When I saw her, I knew I had to make her my wife."

Abigail laughed, her eyes crinkling. "He was so determined to get me to say 'yes' while we were courting. I'm so excited for the wedding."

Uriah slid his arm around her waist with ease, the gesture tender and filled with promise. "I was so happy when she did. I never thought someone like Abigail would want to marry a guy like me."

"Well, I'm glad she did," Winston said, giving Uriah a knowing nod.

"We're all glad she did," came a voice from behind them.

A man in his late twenties strode up and placed a hand on each of their shoulders. He carried a glass of whiskey in one hand and wore an irreverent grin on his lips. Matthew Brown — Abigail's older brother. His presence, like the drink in his hand, seemed both at ease and a touch rebellious, an energy that seemed to ripple through the room as he approached.

"So nice of you to come down and join us, Matthew," Mabel said, her tone betraying a hint of disapproval, her voice clipped, as though she had heard this particular greeting too many times before. She looked at him from under the slant of her brows, her eyes sharp with a mother's concern.

"Oh, I wouldn't miss all this for the world, Mother," Matthew replied, his voice laced with a raised brow, clearly amused by the proceedings. The words were delivered with a smoothness, a nonchalance that suggested he might be enjoying the mild discomfort he was causing.

"Matthew was going to school up North," Winston added, trying to steer the conversation back into familiar territory, "but has unexpectedly come home." There was a pause, the meaning of 'unexpectedly' hanging in the air.

"I was studying to be a doctor," Matthew said with a nonchalant lift of his glass, as if toasting the statement with an air of casual detachment, one hand lazily swirling the whiskey. The words were clearly meant to impress, but the tone suggested he didn't mind leaving it behind.

Jack and Marion exchanged a brief glance, their interest piqued. Both were impressed by the academic accomplishment, but it was Matthew's lack of enthusiasm for it that made it even more intriguing. The decision to leave his studies behind, for reasons yet unknown, was not lost on them.

"I simply needed a break," Matthew added with a casual shrug, as if stepping away from medical studies were no more serious than taking a walk in the park. The indifference in his voice rang out clearly, and it was hard to tell if he was entirely sincere or just playing the role of the aloof young man who had all the answers.

Winston's jaw tightened slightly, a telltale sign of the growing unease. "A break that won't last too long. Right, son?" His voice carried a weight of concern beneath the facade of the fatherly reprimand, the tone that of someone accustomed to trying to steer the course of a rebellious streak.

"No, Dad," Matthew replied smoothly, his voice dripping with ease. "Not long at all." His gaze was calm, steady, though there was something in his demeanor that suggested an unspoken rebellion. He wasn't about to let anyone believe he was staying for long, and yet, there was no denying the sense that he would remain just long enough to make his presence known.

He turned to Uriah, who had been standing quietly at the side, watching the exchange with growing curiosity. Matthew's face softened slightly, but there was a seriousness in his eyes as he looked at Uriah. He reached out and placed one hand on Uriah's shoulder, his grip firm yet affectionate, a subtle gesture of both protection and challenge.

"Just make sure you take care of my sister, Uriah," Matthew said, his voice steady but with an underlying weight to it. "I don't know what

I'd do without her." The affection he had for Abigail was clear in his eyes, but there was something else beneath it—something deeper, more protective, and maybe even possessive.

Abigail, standing beside Uriah, seemed visibly moved by her brother's words. She reached out with a quiet smile, her voice soft but full of warmth. "Thank you, Matthew. I don't know what to say." Her gratitude was genuine, though there was a slight tension in her expression, as though she was caught between her brother's protective nature and her own desire for independence.

Matthew gave a small, affectionate grin before turning back to his father. "I'm sure Uriah will make a fine husband," Winston interjected, his voice firm and full of fatherly pride, though his words carried an air of diplomacy, as if he, too, was hoping to smooth things over.

"Thank you, sir," Uriah said, his voice sincere. "Nothing would make me happier." His words were earnest, and it was clear he respected both Abigail and her family deeply.

Marion, watching the scene unfold before her, exchanged a look with Jack. They both recognized the earnestness in Uriah's tone, but there was something else there too — a touch of youthful dramatics, the kind that came with being a young man at the edge of his future, trying to prove himself in ways that sometimes felt a bit too rehearsed. Still, Marion's smile was kind when she addressed him.

"That's very kind, Uriah," Marion said with a teasing smile, her tone lighthearted. "By the way, that's quite a name." She let the words hang in the air for a moment, her expression playful as she waited for his response.

Uriah blinked at her, slightly taken aback by the sudden attention. "Thank you," he said, his brow furrowing as he tried to make sense of her words, his confusion evident in the way his gaze shifted from Marion to Jack and back.

"Your middle name wouldn't happen to be Heep, would it?" she asked, her lips twitching with amusement, her eyes dancing with a quiet joke that only she seemed to be in on. It was clear that he didn't get the reference to the character written by Dickens. The reference was an old literary one, but it seemed a playful jab.

Uriah blinked again, momentarily lost by the reference, and then replied, "No, ma'am." He paused, clearly trying to decipher the joke, but finding no immediate way to do so. "I'm afraid it's not."

"I was only joking, dear," Marion added quickly, her voice softening when she realized her playful tone hadn't landed quite as expected. There was a brief silence, the air hanging heavy with unspoken tension as Uriah's expression faltered. His eyes briefly flashed something unreadable, a momentary slip of vulnerability, before his smile returned — slightly strained, like a mask hastily put back into place.

Before the awkward silence could stretch any further, Mabel's voice came swiftly to bridge the pause, her tone warm but rushed. "Let me introduce you two to everyone — " she began, eager to move the conversation along and spare everyone further discomfort.

But before she could finish her sentence, Winston gave a sudden groan and placed his hand over his heart, his face contorting with discomfort.

Mabel froze, her eyes widening in sudden concern. "What's wrong?" she asked, her voice rising ever so slightly, her worry unmistakable. She stepped toward her husband, her maternal instincts kicking in.

Winston's face turned pale for a moment, but he quickly brushed the concern aside with a dismissive wave of his hand. "It's nothing," he muttered, his words clipped as he tried to downplay the situation. "Just a little chest pain, nothing to worry about."

Mabel wasn't fooled. She stepped closer, her eyes narrowing with that brand of love and worry only years of shared life could produce. "It's not nothing," she countered, her voice low but firm, thick with concern. "Perhaps you should sit down and take it easy, like Dr. Ritter instructed."

Jack, who had been watching the scene from across the room, already sensing something off, looked over at the exchange. "Everything alright, Winston?" he asked, his tone a mix of casual concern and curiosity.

Winston straightened up a bit, trying to regain his composure. He pushed himself upright, attempting to look more put-together than he felt. "Yes, yes," he said quickly, attempting to reassure everyone, though his voice lacked its usual confidence. "It's just my heart. Some chest pain I've been having lately. Nothing to worry about." The words came out as if he was trying to convince himself more than anyone else.

But Mabel wouldn't let him off so easily. She stepped forward, her eyes searching his face, her concern unwavering. "It most certainly is something to worry about," she said, her voice tinged with quiet insistence.

"Don't make such a fuss," Winston said, offering a half-smile, though it was thin and lacking its usual warmth. "I'm fine. No use in spoiling everybody's fun." He puffed up a little, straightening his shoulders as though physically pushing away the weakness clinging to him. He made a casual wave of his hand as if dismissing it entirely. "See there?" he added with a nonchalant gesture. "It's gone." But his face still looked pale, and his eyes didn't quite hold the same conviction as his words.

Mabel wasn't buying it. She narrowed her eyes at Winston in that way only a longtime spouse could—a mixture of love, suspicion, and exasperation—before shaking her head slightly. It was the kind of look that only someone who had shared years of life with another could truly understand, one that spoke of a thousand little moments of intimate knowing. This was not the first time she had seen him try to dismiss something that was clearly bothering him. The worried furrow in her brow softened just enough to reveal the depth of her concern beneath the layers of patience she had learned to maintain. Her voice, when it came, was firm yet gentle.

"You may be able to fool the others, Winston," she said quietly, her gaze still fixed on him, "but you won't fool me."

Without another word, she turned away, taking a small step back and guiding Jack and Marion away from the scene, her movements graceful but purposeful. The warmth of the gathering seemed to momentarily fade as she led them through the room. The murmur of conversations filled the air like a soft, distant hum, but Mabel's mind was elsewhere, already shifting into hostess mode as she wove through the clusters of guests. She stopped by a couple seated comfortably on a plush velvet couch, their presence like an anchor in the midst of the elegant chaos.

The couple, both in their early sixties, immediately lit up at the sight of Mabel. The woman was African American, soft around the edges, and plump with cheeks that radiated a kind of maternal warmth. Her eyes sparkled with kindness, the sort of person who made you feel like you were the most important person in the room simply by her attention. Her name was Sarah Stevens. Beside her sat her husband George, who, though older and a bit more reserved, exuded a quiet kind of strength. His pale skin, nearly luminous in its contrast to the dim lighting of the parlor, made him stand out, though his presence had a subdued power to it. George was an African American man with albinism, and there was a peaceful, almost meditative calm to him, as though the weight of life's struggles had long since been worn down into quiet acceptance.

"Sarah, George," Mabel said warmly, her voice carrying that familiar lilt of genuine affection. "I'd like you to meet some old friends of ours. This is Jack and Marion Franklin."

The introductions were brief but warm, filled with the kind of politeness that only old friends could manage, the kind of ease that made everything feel effortless. Hands were shaken firmly, smiles were exchanged, and there was that subtle unspoken understanding that these weren't just people Mabel had invited — these were friends. Friends who had been a part of her life for a long time.

"It's about time we had some more people to liven up this party," George said, his gravelly voice breaking through the chatter. His words were good-natured, but there was an unmistakable sense of humor to his tone. It was clear he was someone who enjoyed the company of others, even if his manner was quieter than most.

"Oh, George, listen at you!" Sarah said, nudging him lightly with a soft laugh. "He always says the first thing that pops in his head. Don't pay him no mind, child." There was a twinkle of mischief in her eyes, but she said it with the warmth of a woman who had long ago learned to love her husband's quirks.

George, for his part, grinned at Jack and Marion, and with a mock-serious tone, he added, "Yes, probably for the best," as if proudly confirming the mischief he had caused. His grin only widened as he took in the looks of amusement from the others, his eyes twinkling with the joy of someone who had gotten away with a harmless little jab.

Laughter passed among them like a shared secret, the kind that only happens when familiarity is so deep that no explanation is necessary. It was the laughter of old friends, the kind that had passed between them many times before, each chuckle laced with the memory of years gone by.

Mabel, ever the gracious host, turned to lead Jack and Marion toward two younger guests standing nearby. A girl and a boy — no older than nineteen. The girl, Mary Hart, had bouncy curls that were pinned with care to frame her face, soft and delicate, yet full of youthful energy. The boy beside her was taller, his hair slightly tousled and his posture slightly hunched in a way that suggested he was still growing into his own body. He wore thick glasses that seemed to add an extra layer of self-awareness to his demeanor, the kind of look that young men often adopt when they are trying just a little too hard to appear older than they feel.

"And this," Mabel said, gesturing toward them, "is Mary Hart and Jim Moore. Mary's a student at Spelman. Jim attends Atlanta Baptist College — you know, the young men's school." Her smile was warm as she introduced the young couple, the pride in her voice apparent. It was clear these two were more than just acquaintances to Mabel — they were part of her extended circle.

Jim, adjusting his glasses slightly, looked toward Jack and Marion as if to offer a greeting. "Actually, President Hope is thinking about changing the name of the school," he said with a proud little nod, his voice carrying the excitement of someone who felt involved in something larger than himself.

"Oh really?" Jack asked, intrigued. "To what?" His curiosity was genuine, the question coming from a place of real interest. It wasn't often that one got to hear about changes of this magnitude, and the idea of a school altering its name seemed both significant and curious.

"Morehouse College," Jim replied with a proud little nod, clearly excited by the news. It was as though he were sharing a piece of history in the making, the weight of the moment not lost on him.

"Ah," Jack said, a smile curling at the corners of his lips. "Well, it's nice to meet you both." His voice carried a quiet admiration, impressed not just by the news but by Jim's confidence in sharing it.

89

"What brings you two here?" Marion inquired, her tone genuinely curious. She had been listening to their conversation with interest, and now, as the new guests stood before her, she was eager to learn more about them.

"Mrs. Brown was kind enough to invite us," Mary replied, her voice crisp with gratitude. It was clear from her tone that she was appreciative of the invitation, though she wasn't quite accustomed to such gatherings yet.

"Mr. Brown's a good friend of my dad," Jim added, his voice thoughtful. "He thought it'd be good for my cousin Mary and me to break away from studying for a while."

"Just for tonight, anyway," Mary echoed with a soft laugh, her voice light and easy, as though she were already at ease with the crowd around her.

Mabel nodded toward another cluster of guests. "Now, you may know this next person if you've ever picked up a newspaper." Her voice had shifted into the familiar, enthusiastic tone of someone who had great pride in introducing a distinguished guest.

Mary and Jim drifted off to join George and Sarah, leaving Jack and Marion to follow Mabel toward two sharply dressed men near the corner. One wore a reverend's collar, his posture as straight as a ruler, a White man in his thirties with neatly combed brown hair and the kind of upright poise that came from spending a life behind pulpits. The other was an older African American man — tall and serious-looking, with a receding hairline that only added to his gravitas. His suit fit him perfectly, as though it had been tailored not just to his body, but to his presence. Though he didn't speak right away, the way he stood, the way the air around him seemed to shift, suggested that he commanded the space with quiet authority.

"Mr. Johnson, Reverend John Meadows," Mabel said, her smile broadening. "These are two great friends of ours — Jack and Marion Franklin." She introduced them with ease, her voice warm with familiarity.

As hands were extended and greetings exchanged, Marion froze for a second. Recognition dawned in her eyes as she took in the taller man's face, her pulse quickening with excitement.

91

"I've seen you in the paper," she said, her voice a little breathless. There was a note of surprise and admiration in her tone, the recognition in her eyes unmistakable.

Jack turned to her, puzzled. "You know him, Marion?" His brow furrowed, trying to understand the connection.

"Why of course!" Marion said, her voice rising with polite excitement. "You're Mr. James Weldon Johnson, aren't you?" Her eyes were wide with the sudden realization that she was standing before someone whose name she had read about, whose words had echoed through the pages of history. The honor was apparent in her voice.

The taller man chuckled lightly, a smile playing at the corners of his lips. "Guilty as charged," he said, his voice rich with humility. There was a quiet warmth in his laugh, as though he was accustomed to such recognition but never grew tired of it.

"It's such an honor to meet you, sir," Marion said, her voice firm with respect as she took his hand in a firm handshake. The weight of the moment was not lost on her. She had read about him in the paper, but standing here before him, it felt real in a way that words on a page never could.

"I'll leave you to it," Mabel said, her voice light and gracious. "I have to check on the dinner." With a final smile, she drifted away, leaving Jack and Marion with their new acquaintance.

Once she was gone, James turned back to the group, his smile still warm. "Thank you very much, Mrs. Franklin. It's nice meeting you both as well," he said, his tone genuine. "I was just telling Reverend Meadows how good it feels to get away — despite the circumstances." He added the last words softly, with a slight note of wistfulness, as though the joy of the evening couldn't completely erase the sadness that lay beneath.

"Circumstances?" Jack asked, his eyebrow raised in curiosity, sensing there was more to the story.

James offered a soft, almost nostalgic smile. "Yes, I'm here visiting the family of an old mentor. He passed recently." His voice grew quieter, and there was a brief pause as if the words themselves carried weight. "He was a good man. Helped me become who I am today." The sincerity in his voice was clear, and though his words were humble, there was an undeniable gravity to them.

"Oh," Marion said, her smile dimming slightly with empathy. "I'm so sorry to hear that."

"Thank you," James said, nodding solemnly. "He was a good man. I owe much of who I am to his guidance."

Reverend Meadows, who had been silent up until now, spoke up in a low, reverent tone. "A life well spent awaits a just reward in heaven," he said, his words heavy with the wisdom of someone who had likely seen a lifetime of suffering and triumph.

"Thank you, Reverend," James replied, his eyes flickering with gratitude at the reverent words. "Despite the reason for being here, it's comforting to see so many familiar faces. It's good to be back in Atlanta."

Before the conversation could drift further, a smooth voice cut in from nearby. "You mean away from your responsibilities as a diplomat?"

As the lively chatter filled the parlor, an almost magnetic presence emerged from the crowd. A figure moved through the gathering with a fluid grace, drawing the attention of those around her without needing to announce her arrival. Grace Nail Johnson, striking in her late twenties, moved with an effortless charm that made it appear as though she was meant to glide through the room rather than walk. Her poise was nothing short of polished, and there was a subtle elegance in her every step. Her words, when she spoke, carried the unmistakable rhythm of a New York accent — a soft, lilting cadence that lent an air of refinement to everything she said. It was clear that Grace was a woman who knew the art of making an impression. At her side, with a quiet strength that matched her own presence, was a well-dressed man. Albert Oliver, also in his late twenties, walked with a confidence that could not be shaken, despite the cane he carried. His posture was erect, a reflection of someone who had learned to carry himself well, despite the challenges he may have faced. There was an unspoken steadiness in him, an almost unshakable confidence in the way he moved, a calmness that contrasted with the more vibrant energy around him.

As the two approached, James, who had been speaking with Reverend Meadows, gestured toward them, his smile widening as he introduced the newcomers. "That is precisely what I mean," James said, his voice still warm with the ease of the conversation. "Mr. and Mrs. Franklin, this is my wife, Grace."

Grace extended her hand with an elegant smile that seemed to draw the light of the room to her. "It's a pleasure to meet you both," she said, her voice warm but with a subtle sophistication. There was no rush in her movements, no indication of hurry. She allowed the moment to linger, just long enough to make Jack and Marion feel not only welcomed but valued. After a brief handshake, she turned her attention back to Albert, her smile widening ever so slightly. "By the way, where are my manners?" she said with a touch of playful self-awareness. "This clever man here is Albert Oliver. Mr. Oliver was just telling me the most delightful story."

Albert, ever the gentleman, offered a modest grin, the kind that suggested amusement but not arrogance. "Well, it won't leave you in stitches, but it'll pass the time until dinner is served. How do you do, Mr. and Mrs. Franklin?" His voice was calm, with a richness to it that suggested he was used to being in the company of well-spoken people but had no intention of letting that make him seem distant.

Another round of handshakes followed, and Grace, her eyes twinkling with the familiarity of a longtime partnership, added, "I tease my husband all the time," her hand gently resting on James's arm. The affection was subtle but unmistakable. "But he's right. It's such a good feeling to get away from the confines of Nicaragua where he's stationed."

Reverend Meadows, who had been observing the exchange, raised an amused brow, as if sensing an opportunity for humor. "Don't tell me the duties of a U.S. consul are getting to you, Mr. Johnson! Weren't you appointed under Theodore Roosevelt?" His voice carried an undercurrent of amusement, as if he'd known James for long enough to make such lighthearted jabs without offense.

"Yes," James replied with a chuckle, clearly enjoying the exchange. "But I've made more progress under the current administration. The opposing parties in the Nicaraguan Congress have agreed to put aside their differences. Their country supports a new constitution— though we'll see how long that endures." His voice held a note of cautious optimism, a reflection of the delicate and often unpredictable nature of international relations.

97

Grace turned her eyes to him with admiration, her gaze softening as she listened to her husband speak. "If anyone can assist them in such a feat, it's you," she said, her voice infused with the kind of belief that only a wife could carry. There was no doubt in her tone, no hesitation. It was the simple, unspoken confidence of someone who had seen their partner overcome obstacles before and knew they would again.

James smiled warmly, his expression softening in a way that suggested deep affection. He leaned toward Grace, placing a gentle kiss on her cheek. "Thank you," he whispered, though his words were meant for only her, the rest of the room filled with the kind of understanding that needed no explanation.

Jack, having been listening to the conversation with interest, leaned forward slightly, a thoughtful expression crossing his face. "Have you gained a lot from the culture there?" he asked, his curiosity evident. It wasn't just an idle question—Jack had always been one to seek out deeper meanings in new experiences, and the opportunity to learn from someone who had been immersed in another culture for a long period intrigued him.

"Most definitely!" James answered without hesitation, his enthusiasm clear. Then, with a swift, fluid motion, he broke into Spanish, the words flowing easily from him. "Estar con amigos es ser feliz!" His tone was warm, as if the phrase itself carried a piece of the happiness he had found there, among his friends.

Marion blinked in slight confusion. "What does that mean?" she asked, her voice gentle, though the curiosity was evident.

"To be with friends is to be happy!" James translated with a smile, his tone sincere and open, as if inviting Marion—and anyone else listening—to join in the joy that the phrase symbolized.

Laughter rippled through the group, like a wave that carried the warmth of the moment deeper into the hearts of everyone present. There was something comforting in the way they all shared the moment—laughter, language, and the simple joy of each other's company—drawing them closer together, creating an unspoken bond that would linger long after the evening ended.

Meanwhile, in a quieter corner of the room, students Mary Hart and Jim Moore settled into an easy conversation with the elderly couple,

George and Sarah Stevens. The two young students, so full of life and curiosity, had quickly warmed to the more seasoned couple, their questions coming easily as they sought to learn more about the lives of those who had lived through decades of change.

"How do you know the Browns, Mrs. Stevens?" Mary asked, her voice soft but interested, eager to learn more about the people around her.

Sarah chuckled lightly, her eyes twinkling with good-natured warmth. "Oh, please, call me Sarah," she said with a soft laugh. "We know them from church. The Browns are kind people, always welcoming."

"They sure are," George agreed, his voice deep and steady, as he settled back into the armchair, folding his hands over his belly with the ease of someone who had long since grown accustomed to a comfortable, reliable life. He let out a long, almost theatrical sigh, his tone shifting to something more reflective. "Boy, today sure was a hard day," he said, as though the weight of the day's events still lingered on his mind.

"It sure was," Sarah echoed, her voice full of empathy, as she too seemed to reflect on the day's challenges.

Mary, sensing a moment of shared understanding, leaned in slightly. "What do you do, Sarah?" she asked, genuinely interested in hearing more about the life of this kind woman who had given so much of herself to others.

"I'm a midwife," Sarah replied, her voice strong, though there was a hint of weariness in it. "So I'm always on the go. And George here is a laborer on the railroad."

She gestured affectionately to her husband, her eyes filled with pride.

Jim, his tone turning thoughtful, asked, "Do you ever feel like quitting it?"

George barked a laugh, a sharp but friendly sound that drew a chuckle from those nearby. "Hell no!" he exclaimed, his voice filled with an almost boisterous confidence.

"Why not?" Jim asked, a grin tugging at the corners of his lips, intrigued by the boldness in George's response.

George straightened slightly in his chair, a glimmer of pride flashing in his eyes. "Because it's a good thing to work," he said, his tone firm and no-nonsense. "There's nothing wrong with workin', young buck. Especially if the work is honest." There was a finality to his words, as though the matter was settled in his mind. Work was honorable, and that was all there was to it.

Mary leaned in, curiosity still piqued. "What if they decide not to be honest?" she asked, her voice taking on a thoughtful, almost philosophical tone.

George tilted his head slightly, his brow furrowing in slight confusion. "What do you mean?" he asked, genuinely unsure where the conversation was going.

"What if they decide one day not to show up with the money?" Mary pressed gently, her question becoming more pointed, more curious.

George didn't miss a beat. He tilted his head back slightly, his gaze steady, before responding with a wink and a smile. "Then that's the day I won't show up," he said simply, his voice full of unshakable confidence.

The room erupted in laughter, loud and unfiltered. The sound was contagious, each person's laughter mingling with the others, the shared joy infectious. George, pointing at Jim with a grin, added, "You hear me, Jim? And that's me just being honest." His words, though playful, carried an undeniable weight — a life lived with authenticity, with integrity, and without compromise.

On the opposite side of the room, Reverend Meadows, Marion, Albert, James, Grace, and Jack were deep in conversation. Their voices rose and fell with ease, as the group became absorbed in discussion, but there was still a sense of underlying tension in Albert's gaze.

"How do you know the Browns, Albert?" Reverend Meadows asked, his voice filled with curiosity.

"Are you a relative?" Marion added, her tone friendly but inquisitive.

Albert offered a half-smile, his posture just a touch more guarded. "No, I'm Uriah's brother," he said, his words flowing smoothly, though there was a subtle tension in his voice. "He invited me. I suppose he thought I might enjoy gettin' out of the house."

103

Marion nodded understandingly, a sympathetic smile on her face. "It's so nice to get out for once and be free," she said, her voice light but laced with a quiet truth.

The group murmured in agreement, but Albert's gaze dropped slightly, a flicker of something deeper crossing his expression. "Not all of us are free, Mrs. Franklin," he said quietly.

Just then, as if to shift the mood, Mabel Brown appeared in the doorway, her voice bright and cheerful. "Alright everyone! Dinner is served."

The crowd stirred, chairs shuffled, and voices lifted in pleasant conversation. Everyone began moving toward the dining room, the air thick with anticipation and hunger. Amid the crowd, Uriah and Albert were the last to leave the parlor.

Albert hesitated, his hand reaching to rest on Uriah's arm. "I don't know about this, Uriah. What are we thinking?"

Uriah's face twisted into something resembling amusement, but his tone held none of the same clarity. "Don't get cold feet on me now, brother," he said, his voice low, steady. "It's just a game."

Albert stared at him, voice tight. "What? Is that what you think this is — a game?"

Uriah chuckled, but there was no humor in the sound.

It was dark, almost hollow. "Of course."

Then, with a sudden shift, his voice dropped lower, the words heavier. "Our situation is bad, Albert. Mama's sick. Her doctor bills keep piling up. Daddy can't find a job. He drinks away every spare penny he makes. This is for us — for our family."

Albert's voice cracked. He stood rooted, his hand still near Uriah's sleeve, as if hoping to stop him with a simple touch. "What you're doing is wrong, Uriah. Love ain't no game, you know."

Uriah stiffened, his eyes narrowing. "Who said anything about love?"

With that, he pulled away, his face unreadable, and walked from the room, leaving Albert behind — uncertain, conflicted, heavy-hearted.

Just as Albert turned to follow, a quiet movement stirred behind him. He looked up — and there was Abigail, standing in the hallway. She hadn't said a word, but she had heard everything. Her eyes searched his, serious and full of unspoken questions. Albert's chest tightened. He couldn't speak.

Without a word, he turned away and walked on toward the dining room. Moments later, Abigail followed — her footsteps quiet, deliberate, and full of meaning.

CHAPTER 6

MARION

The grand dining room of the Brown residence shimmered beneath the golden luminescence of the chandelier, its light spilling in cascading warmth across polished mahogany and gleaming silverware. The long table — draped in a pristine white cloth and flanked by high-backed chairs — stretched like a regal bridge between the guests, bearing a feast fit for kings: roasted meats fragrant with herbs and fat, vegetables lacquered in honeyed glaze, golden-crusted breads still warm from the oven, and crystal decanters of deep red wine that caught the light like liquid garnet. For a moment, no one moved. There was a reverent stillness, as if the splendor before them demanded a quiet acknowledgement before indulgence.

Marion Franklin clasped her hands with audible delight. "Oh, Mabel! Everything looks simply wonderful."

Mabel Brown's face flushed with a deep, satisfied glow. She nodded with modest pride, brushing a nonexistent crease from her dress as she took in the guests' awestruck faces. "Thank you, Marion. I do hope you all came with your appetites. Please — take your seats."

Chairs scraped softly against the floor as the guests obliged, their voices lowering to a murmur as they arranged themselves around the table. Winston Brown moved with unhurried purpose to the seat at the head, his presence stately but not self-important, a man used to command and quiet reverence. Mabel settled beside him, her bearing graceful, her smile gracious yet watchful — like a hostess who knew the delicate balance between hospitality and control.

She leaned in, her voice low but unmistakably coaxing. "Shouldn't you say something, dear?"

Winston straightened, his tall frame unfolding from the chair like a soldier rising to deliver command. He lifted a slim glass of wine, its contents catching the light, and his voice rang out with a quiet authority that stilled the remaining whispers in the room.

"I'd like to show my gratitude to you all for joining us this evening," he began, his gaze sweeping slowly over the room, stopping for a moment on each familiar face. "Tonight reminds me of the power of three things — things too often taken for granted in this world. The first is family. The second is friendship." He paused deliberately, his eyes now resting on his daughter Abigail, seated radiant and poised beside her fiancé, Uriah. "And the third — perhaps the most enduring of all — is love."

A gentle wave of smiles and nods rippled across the table. There was something tender in the way the light played across Abigail's face as she looked at Uriah, her fingers resting delicately on the table's edge, her posture proud yet deferential, as if trying to live up to the moment. Most of the room watched them with fondness. All except Albert, whose gaze remained hard and inscrutable, his glass untouched.

Winston raised his own higher. "So, I'd like to make a toast," he said, pausing once more to gather weight behind his words. "To Uriah and my lovely daughter Abigail. May their future be long, bright, and steadfast."

The guests responded with a warm chorus of "To Uriah and Abigail!" as glasses were lifted, clinked, and sipped.

The feast began in earnest. Silver cutlery clinked gently against china, and the warm hum of conversation resumed, less formal now, more free-flowing. James Weldon Johnson leaned over toward Winston, his voice low with a note of gratitude. "Thank you very much for inviting my wife and me to share in this celebration."

Winston waved the thanks away with a casual flick of the wrist. "Think nothing of it," he said. "You're a dear friend, James. We've come a long way together."

Sarah Stevens, further down the table, added brightly, "That was such a lovely speech, Winston. Abigail, you're a lucky gal."

George grunted in agreement as he cut into his roast with the practiced ease of a man who'd eaten his share of celebratory meals. "Ain't it the truth? We should all speak our hearts a little more—say what we mean to the people we love before it's too late."

Mary, unusually quiet, nodded solemnly, her hands resting in her lap. "I agree with that, Mr. Stevens. I'd give anything just to speak to my father again."

Marion turned toward her, a gentle crease forming between her brows. "What do you mean?"

Mary's voice grew softer, more reflective. "My father died a few years ago."

"I'm sorry to hear that," Winston said immediately, his rich voice dipping with genuine sympathy.

Mary offered a small, polite smile, but her eyes had lost their luster, turned inward. "Thank you," she said, then hesitated. Jack, ever young and unfiltered, leaned forward, curiosity overtaking his caution.

"How did he die?" he asked.

A quiet settled over the table. Marion shot him a withering look—sharp enough to pierce—but Mary lifted her hand gently, forgiving. "No, it's alright," she said, her gaze now distant. "He was one of the many who died in 1906…during the riot. We were visiting my aunt in Macon. My mother, my brothers, and I. My father stayed home. He didn't think the trouble would come so far. But when it came, he was alone." Everyone remembered that horrible disaster all those years ago in 1906, when those mobs of white men came to Auburn Avenue to burn it down – all over terrible lies.

George's face darkened, his knife pausing mid-slice. "That whole thing was terrible. Unforgivable."

Winston's jaw tightened. His voice, when it came, was low and controlled, but with a hard steel edge. "The newspapers called it a riot. Let's call it what it was — a massacre."

"A massacre that didn't need to happen," Marion murmured, her eyes low. "So many innocent lives."

The air grew heavier, the food momentarily forgotten. Then Jim, who'd been quiet until now, spoke with a narrowed gaze. His words were calm, but carried the chill of accusation. "And where were you that night, Reverend Meadows? You know… when all of that happened."

The shift in the room was immediate and palpable. It was as if someone had opened a door and let winter in. Reverend Meadows blinked, caught in the sudden spotlight, and Winston's posture turned rigid with disapproval.

"I wasn't in Atlanta at the time," the reverend said evenly. "I was studying with the clergy in Philadelphia."

"But what if you had been?" Matthew's voice now joined the fray — cool, curious, dangerous.

Albert leaned in slightly, his voice low but sharp.

"Yeah. What would you have done then?"

Before the tension could peak, Mabel's voice cut through the air like a bell. "Gentlemen, please! Reverend Meadows is a guest at our table. I won't have him interrogated."

But the reverend held up a hand, his tone quiet and firm. "It's alright, Mrs. Brown," he said. His gaze moved back to the young men. "If I had been here... I wouldn't have been among the fifteen thousand White men who took to the streets with fists and guns. I assure you. I would've been standing with my brethren who needed defending."

Matthew tilted his head, skeptical. "Oh, really?"

"Yes," the reverend said, meeting his gaze squarely. "Really."

Another pause. Tighter this time. Then Matthew leaned back, smirking slightly, his voice dropping.

"Well, at least we know we've got an ally in the room. Unlike some of those white folks at your church."

The implication hung in the air. Reverend Meadows opened his mouth, but Winston raised a hand — this time with a tight, barely controlled fury.

"Can we drop this subject, please?" he said, jaw clenched.

Abigail, who had remained composed until now, turned to Matthew with an icy glare. "Matthew, please act like you've got some home training."

Matthew shrugged with faux innocence. "What? At least we know the reverend's not a murderer."

"Matthew!" Mabel snapped, scandalized.

But he pressed on. "Not like the one that's still out there."

Every fork froze. Wine paused midway to mouths.

Conversation died.

"The one who's already taken eight victims," Matthew continued, voice low and deliberate. "The Atlanta Constitution offered a reward just this morning. They're calling him the Atlanta Ripper now."

He said the name like it tasted of smoke and iron.

"That's enough," Winston growled, but Matthew ignored him.

"You know," he added, tone almost playful now, "like the one in London? Back in the 1880s? They never caught him either."

Then he drew a slow finger across his throat. "From ear to ear…"

Winston's chair screeched across the floor as he stood abruptly, towering above the table. His eyes blazed.

"That is enough!"

A hush fell like a curtain. The only sound was the distant ticking of the grandfather clock in the hallway.

"This night is supposed to be special — for your sister," Winston continued, voice taut with fury. "And I will not allow you to soil it with your foolishness."

Matthew said nothing. His smirk had vanished.

Winston exhaled, adjusted his coat, and sat again, the gesture smooth but weighted. "If you cannot behave," he said quietly, "I suggest you excuse yourself. Otherwise, keep silent."

Matthew looked around the room — at the stunned expressions, at his mother's heartbreak, at Abigail's fury. At the heat rising in his father's eyes. Silently, he picked up his fork and resumed eating, not another word spoken.

Trying to ease the tension, Marion turned with deliberate lightness to Abigail. "So, Abigail," she said, her voice gentle but firm, "how did you and Uriah come to know each other?"

Abigail drew a breath, sat taller. Her smile emerged slowly, carefully formed, as though built from porcelain. "Well," she said sweetly, "it's a funny story…"

As her voice filled the space, the room began to breathe again. But something had changed. The shadows had lengthened. Tension hung in the corners like cobwebs, and the wind outside whispered against the windows like a ghost rattling to be let in.

The candles burned steady and bright, but everyone at the table knew — somewhere, out beyond the warm glow of crystal and glass, something was stirring in the dark.

CHAPTER 7

JACK

The foyer of the Brown residence had quieted to a low murmur, the kind of hush that settles after a sumptuous meal when the clinking of glasses and the cadence of laughter begin to dissolve into the softer rhythms of digestion and post-dinner reflection. The once-vibrant dining room now echoed with the fading sounds of retreating footsteps, shoes brushing against polished floors, and voices melting into a melodic hum somewhere beyond the parlor. The scent of roast duck and seasoned root vegetables still lingered faintly in the air, mingling with the fragrance of polished mahogany and a subtle waft of Mabel's rose water perfume.

Beneath the glow of the sconce lights, golden and warm against the amber-toned wood paneling — Winston Brown remained behind, his tall figure shadowed against the grand staircase. A man of stature and calculation, he moved with deliberate care, one hand in his pocket, the other reaching to rest lightly on Reverend Meadows's elbow. There was no urgency in the gesture, but there was intent. Quiet intent.

"John," he murmured, voice low, steady, and shaped by years of diplomacy. "I'm sorry about my son. He... well, he can be a bit of a rough diamond."

His lips formed a rueful smile, one that didn't quite reach his eyes. The words, though casual on the surface, carried with them the weight of a father's resignation— of a man who had lived long enough to know that not every flaw could be polished out.

Reverend John Meadows, ever composed, responded with a patient nod, the corners of his mouth lifting only slightly. "It's alright, Winston. He still has a lot of growing up to do."

A sigh unfurled from Winston's chest like a draft from an old, reluctant chimney. The kind that takes with it a little warmth, a little hope. "I'm afraid so."

For a moment, they stood together in that vestibule between rooms and expectations, between past and future. The reverend's gaze wandered the length of the hallway, taking in the home's quiet grandeur — the brass fixtures gleaming in the lamplight, the oil paintings of ancestors whose faces watched from above as if still measuring the legacy left in their wake. In the distance, porcelain dishes clinked as the staff cleared away the remnants of the meal, their quiet movements a respectful echo of the evening's earlier celebration.

"Things seem to be going quite well for you," Meadows observed, his tone casual, but his eyes scanning with more than passing interest. "The insurance company you founded is doing very well, I see."

Winston's expression brightened, if only briefly. A flicker of pride rose behind his usually stoic exterior. "Yes, it's done well. Better than I ever expected, truth be told. We've grown rapidly. And, thankfully, not a single complaint so far." He gave a pause, then lowered his voice to something gentler, more personal. "But enough about business. How are you, John? I can't imagine passing being easy for you."

At the mention of that word — passing — a faint shadow passed over Meadows's face. His shoulders straightened, spine taut as if bracing against an invisible wind. His response came clipped, measured. "No, it isn't."

There was a silence then. Not uncomfortable, but weighty. A shared silence between men who understood the costs of survival in a divided world.

"You're working for a noble cause," Winston said, trying perhaps to steer them back to solid ground. "What's the name of that group again?"

"The National Association for the Advancement of Colored People," Meadows replied with quiet pride. "NAACP. It's only been around for two years, but we're growing."

Winston nodded, his brow creasing slightly in thought. "Yes, yes — that's right. I read something recently in their publication The Crisis. There was a note about Harriet Tubman — how she's being moved to the home she founded in

Rochester. Her final years..." His voice faltered a little, as though the name itself demanded a reverence no words could fully meet. "Poor woman."

The weight of history hung between them. There were no further words needed. The silence that followed was reverent, lined with the ghosts of freedom fighters, lynched souls, and women like Harriet who had carried generations on their backs.

"She's endured so much," Winston added softly.

Meadows nodded slowly. "The NAACP's mission is to uplift our people, Winston. Negroes all over the country. It's an interracial effort— Black and white working together. Unity is our strength."

Before Winston could reply, a gentle rustle of fabric drew their attention. Mabel appeared at the archway to the parlor, her posture graceful, her smile as soft and reassuring as the notes of a lullaby. The light behind her haloed her in a golden glow.

"Winston, Reverend Meadows...everyone's waiting," she said with her usual warmth. "Jim's about to play something on the piano. Is everything alright?"

Winston, ever the gentleman in moments like these, straightened slightly. "Yes, dear. Everything's fine. We'll be there in a moment."

Reverend Meadows inclined his head politely. "Thank you, Mrs. Brown. Your hospitality tonight has been most gracious."

She returned the gesture with a smile that held the weariness of a hostess near the end of a long evening, and turned, disappearing back into the gentle hum of the parlor. Her scent lingered behind her like an echo.

Winston turned back toward the reverend. His voice dropped, intimate once more. "But why Atlanta?" he asked. "Why would the NAACP send you here, of all places?"

The change in Reverend Meadows was immediate. His features darkened with gravity. His posture grew even stiller. "After national news spread of the massacre, I was sent to act as an influence, a sort of spy if you will, into the White community here. I'm supposed to enter the inner circles and inform the NAACP of any schemes that may hinder or harm local Negroes."

123

"Well, that may prove to be a useful tactic," Winston's tone was encouraging. "After all, it worked for Homer Plessy during his time with the Louisiana Citizens Committee back in the 1890s."

Meadows didn't flinch.

"Yes, but Plessy was arrested. That arrest led to Plessy v. Ferguson, and we both know how that ended."

A heaviness settled over Winston.

"Yes," he said slowly with regret, "we do."

There suddenly was a stillness between them.

"But I keep going," Meadows added, voice tight, eyes distant. "No one here knows why I'm truly in Atlanta. And I intend to keep it that way. Not because I'm ashamed. I'm not. But because I'll do what I must for our people—to see this promise through. Liberty. Justice. Even if I don't live long enough to witness it myself."

There was something in his voice that didn't just speak—it prophesied.

Winston looked at the man in front of him as though truly seeing him for the first time. Not just a preacher. Not just a guest. But something else—

124

a sentinel. He reached out, resting a hand on Meadows's shoulder, then clasped it in a firm, meaningful shake.

"May God be with you, my friend," Winston said, the words heavy with respect.

But before the moment could pass completely, Winston winced, one hand flying instinctively to his chest. His face pinched for a brief second in pain.

"Winston?" Meadows's brow furrowed. "Are you alright?"

"I'm fine," Winston replied quickly, though his voice betrayed him. He attempted a smile, the edges strained. "Just a bit of indigestion, I suppose."

They began to walk slowly toward the parlor.

At that very moment, Abigail emerged from the bathroom down the hall. She paused, catching sight of the two men. Her eyes landed on Reverend Meadows and held there. Something unreadable flickered in her gaze — curiosity, suspicion, or perhaps something deeper and more ancient. Her expression was porcelain-still, her poise intact, but her gaze lingered. And lingered.

Winston, unaware, passed her with a father's weary stride, already halfway into the next room. But Reverend Meadows hesitated. He felt it before he saw it—the subtle prickle of being watched.

He turned his head just slightly, and met her gaze. For a fraction of a second, they stared at one another, neither blinking.

A chill passed between them.

No words were spoken. None were needed. Something had been exchanged—quiet, veiled, unfinished.

Then, without breaking his composure, Reverend Meadows followed Winston into the parlor.

A few moments later, Abigail stepped through the doorway as well.

The parlor, radiant in amber lamplight and polished wood, pulsed with warmth and music. Reverend Meadows and Winston entered to find the air thick with chatter, laughter, and the soft chime of crystal against crystal. Abigail trailed behind them, her footsteps soundless, her presence almost spectral—hovering just beyond reach, like a thought unspoken.

126

At the upright piano, Jim sat poised, his fingers lightly grazing the ivory keys, surrounded by guests who had relaxed into the rhythm of the evening. Near the hearth, James Weldon Johnson and his elegant wife, Grace Nail Johnson, approached Winston with parting smiles.

"Winston," James said, his voice low and gracious, "thank you for the lovely dinner. Grace and I must be going. It's been a beautiful evening."

Grace offered her hand with a warm, practiced elegance. "And many congratulations to your beautiful daughter. Marriage is such a sacred bond. We're truly happy for her."

Winston bowed his head with quiet gratitude. "You're very kind. And I wish the both of you the best of luck overseas." He gestured with a courteous hand. "Allow me to see you out."

Across the room, a ripple of laughter danced over the guests like a rising tide. At the piano, Mary leaned toward Jim and whispered something softly. Jim glanced at her, a grin pulling at the corner of his lips, and gave a subtle nod.

"That's a great idea, cousin," he murmured.

Mary turned just in time to catch James and Grace nearing the door.

"Oh, Mr. and Mrs. Johnson!" she called, her voice ringing clearly through the air. "Please don't leave just yet. We have a surprise for you."

They paused. James tilted his head, a flicker of curiosity in his gaze, already suspecting what she meant. And then Jim's fingers found the first few solemn chords of a melody James knew by heart.

"Lift Every Voice and Sing."

Mary's voice rose above the notes, firm and bright, carrying the opening lines with a poise far beyond her years. Her tone held both reverence and resolve, her presence commanding. The parlor slowly quieted, conversations stilled, and glasses were set aside. The guests leaned in, listening.

One by one, voices joined hers—hesitant at first, then stronger, swelling into a shared harmony. When Mary extended her hand slightly, beckoning more to join, they did. The room transformed into a chorus of faith and defiance, old pain and new hope stitched into every note.

"Let us march on till victory is won…"

The final line rang out like a promise, and then applause thundered through the parlor—raw, unguarded, deeply felt.

James stood still, visibly moved. Moisture shimmered at the edges of his eyes. "Thank you," he said softly, voice trembling with emotion. "That was quite beautiful—one of the best renditions I've heard thus far."

With a tender smile, Grace took his arm. Together, they exited without further delay, Winston trailing just behind to see them to the door.

The parlor, left in their wake, seemed changed. Lighter. As though something sacred had passed through it.

"That truly was splendid," Marion said, her expression proud and bright.

"Great job, darlin'," Sarah added, reaching to squeeze Mary's hand.

Winston returned from the foyer, his mood buoyant.

"I think he enjoyed it, don't you?"

A round of laughter followed.

Jim cracked his knuckles playfully over the keys.

"What should I play next?"

"Something by Scott Joplin?" Jack suggested.

George's eyes sparked with delight. "Perfect! Who doesn't love Maple Leaf Rag or The Entertainer?"

"Alright then," Jim said with a wink, and launched into the sprightly cadence of The Entertainer.

The parlor caught fire again—this time with movement. Shoes tapped, dresses twirled, and bodies gave in to the rhythm. A blur of dance followed: waltzes spun into two-steps, and someone attempted the exuberant Texas Tommy. The room shimmered with color and laughter, every corner brimming with joy.

But not everyone felt the pull of music.

"Excuse me, everyone," Abigail said, her voice slicing through the mirth.

Uriah turned toward her, brow lifting. "Where are you going?"

Her eyes met his with icy precision. "Never you mind."

Without another word, she slipped into the hallway, the soft swish of her skirt vanishing behind her like a closing curtain.

Outside, a sudden boom broke the evening air — the unmistakable burst of fireworks.

"What was that?" Reverend Meadows asked, startled.

Winston turned toward the sound, cheerful. "Looks like they've commenced the fireworks for this evening. Let's all go outside and have a look!"

"Winston, where's your toilet?" Reverend Meadows asked quietly.

"Just around the corner once you exit the parlor."

Meadows offered a quick nod and stepped away. One by one, the guests began to follow Winston, their voices fading into the night, carried by bursts of red, gold, and violet streaking across the sky.

Inside, only Matthew remained.

Winston turned, brows knit. "Aren't you coming along, Matthew?"

Matthew lifted his glass, unconcerned. "No, I think I'll stay behind."

He turned on his heel and disappeared into the shadowed hallway.

Winston lingered for a beat, gaze trailing after him, then shifted to Uriah and Albert.

"What about you and your brother?"

"I'll be out shortly, Mr. Brown," Uriah replied, his voice carefully measured. "I'm going to check on Abigail. See what's taking her so long."

"Same here, Mr. Brown," Albert added quickly, his tone harder, more possessive.

Winston gave a short nod and stepped outside, joining the rest under the flickering sky.

Back in the parlor, silence reclaimed the space. Only Uriah and Albert remained.

Albert's voice was tight. "We're not done with this."

Uriah turned toward him slowly, his eyes sharp.

"Yes, we are."

He strode from the room without hesitation.

Albert followed, jaw clenched, the air behind them thick with something unspoken — something dangerous.

CHAPTER 8

MARION

T he night sky above the Brown residence bloomed with brilliance, a symphony of color and thunder that sent shimmering waves across the lawn and rooftops. Fireworks burst in timed succession, their echoing booms rolling through the humid summer air like distant drums of war. The front lawn had become a gathering of silhouettes—Winston, Mabel, Marion, Jack, Sarah, George, Jim, and Mary— each one bathed in fleeting reds, golds, and indigos as their faces turned upward in collective wonder. Laughter floated like music in the air,

134

harmonizing with the jubilant cries of Black children from nearby porches and the persistent crackle of celebratory sparks. The African American citizens of Auburn Avenue were at the height of exaltation.

Winston stood quietly beside Mabel, his smile gentle, though not entirely at ease. The bursts above reflected in his eyes, but something else lived behind them — an unsettled flicker, barely noticeable to anyone but himself. His fingers curled and uncurled at his sides, like he was waiting for something, though even he could not say what.

"Here it comes!" Jim cried out, and all heads turned toward the sky just as a colossal explosion erupted — a chandelier of golden light that fell in slow, glimmering arcs. Cheers erupted. Applause followed. The joy was palpable.

But inside the house, far from the glow of pyrotechnics and celebration, a different energy pulsed — coiled and sharp.

In the narrow confines of the library, Abigail moved like a trapped animal, her footsteps brisk and erratic as she paced before the wall of old, towering shelves. The low flame of an oil lamp danced upon the polished wood, throwing long shadows that warped with her every movement. Her breath came quick and uneven, her hands jittery as they flew over bindings and spines, yanking volumes loose without thought or care. Each book thudded onto the rug or fell sideways against its neighbors, her desperation growing with every second. The rich scent of aged paper and dust, once a comfort, now clung to her like a shroud.

She wasn't sure what she was looking for—only that she had to find it. Something. Anything. Answers she hadn't known she needed until now.

Then her fingers brushed it: a leather cover, thicker than the others, hidden behind a row of slimmer titles. Her breath caught. With a sharp tug, she pulled it free. The book thudded open against the desk, its pages dry and whispering beneath her trembling touch. She flipped through it rapidly, her eyes scanning in hungry, jerking movements.

And then—there.

Tucked between the brittle pages, almost as if the book had been guarding it, lay a single folded sheet of paper. Her hands closed around it before she'd fully registered the motion. She unfolded it slowly, reverently. Her eyes flicked across its contents, and something inside her shifted. A revelation. A confirmation. Her breath hitched.

"Yes..." she whispered, a word not of victory, but of fragile hope on the edge of collapse. Relief crashed into her like a wave — and just as quickly, receded.

The sound was soft. Barely a murmur above the din of fireworks — but unmistakable.

The creak of a door hinge.

Abigail stiffened. The air in the room thickened. Her hand, still gripping the paper, trembled. She turned her head slowly, not daring to move more than that. The shadows in the doorway shifted.

Then she saw them.

A pair of polished black shoes stepped into view.

That was all she needed.

Her mouth went dry. Her heart began to pound — not with excitement this time, but with a hollow, sickening dread that sank straight into her bones. She didn't need to see the face. The shoes were enough.

"You?" she managed to say, her voice barely more than a breath, raw with disbelief and fear. Her mind scrambled for logic, for safety, for any justification—but none came. Only silence.

The door clicked shut behind the figure, sealing them both inside. The lamplight flickered, casting their shadows into monstrous forms against the walls.

She could hear the soft sound of breathing now. Closer. Measured. Deliberate.

And then the figure stepped forward.

Outside, the crescendo of fireworks reached its thunderous peak, a cataclysm of color and sound erupting against the velvet sky. The heavens themselves seemed to burn as golds, crimsons, and silvers blossomed in furious succession, one after the other, until the very firmament appeared aflame. Each explosion fractured the night with heart-stopping brilliance, sending shudders through the cobbled ground and rattling the windows of every nearby house. Faces in the crowd below turned skyward, bathed in waves of kaleidoscopic light, their expressions aglow with wonder, their cheers rising like a tidal roar in ecstatic unison. For that brief, dazzling moment, the world was caught in suspended awe—its fears drowned beneath a canopy of fire and stars, its secrets lost in the echo of celebration.

But inside the Brown residence, the festivities did not exist.

The glow of the lamplight flickered as if uncertain, wavering against the tension that had settled into the room like a living thing. Abigail stumbled back, the heel of her shoe catching against the ornate rug, her breath fractured and thin, her lungs drawing in air that tasted too sharp, too cold. Her eyes, wide with disbelief, locked onto the face of the figure before her — half-lit, half-shadowed — its features molded into something almost inhuman under the jittering flame. Her hand groped blindly behind her for the edge of the desk, fingers brushing across polished wood, searching, yearning for something solid, something sharp, something that could make sense of the terror blossoming in her chest.

And then—contact. Smooth oak beneath her hand. Hope.

But it vanished the instant she felt it.

A hand, gloved and cold, descended upon her shoulder — firm, resolute, and chilling in its quiet authority. Abigail inhaled sharply, a gasp crushed against the back of her throat, never given the breath to become a scream. She spun to face him fully, her heart pounding a deafening rhythm in her ears. His eyes met hers — two fathomless voids, dark and glacial, so still they seemed beyond emotion, beyond conscience. There was no rage in them, no wildness. Only the calm deliberation of a man who had already decided what came next.

She moved — quick, desperate, darting to her right, the soles of her shoes sliding slightly against the polished wood. But he moved too, with the unerring precision of someone who had done this before. No stumble, no hesitation. Just cold calculation.

Her hand shot out for the door. Fingers skimmed the cold brass handle...

And then he was there.

Between her and freedom. An unmovable wall of darkness that blocked the corridor of escape. His silhouette loomed, swallowing the last sliver of light as his shadow spread outward, devouring everything in its path—until she stood engulfed within it.

Abigail opened her mouth to scream.

But outside, the fireworks screamed louder.

Another explosion, louder than the last, rattled the windowpanes and silenced her cry before it ever reached the world. She tried again, choking on the silence, her voice lodged behind the wall of fear in her throat. Her body tensed, every nerve ablaze, as she took a half-step back.

He did not speak. He didn't need to. The quiet was a blade of its own.

Then—without warning—his hand struck forward.

Something soft pressed against her face. A cloth. Damp. Fragrant. Sickly sweet. She drew in a breath before she could stop herself, and the scent filled her head—cloying and strange, syrupy and sharp. Her eyes went wide in recognition.

Chloroform.

Panic exploded in her veins. She thrashed instinctively, arms flailing, trying to pry him off, to shove him back, to breathe anything but that

141

D.L. JORDAN

poisoned sweetness. Her nails raked against fabric, skin— something. But her strength was failing her already. Her muscles betrayed her, weakening with frightening speed, her body growing heavy, her thoughts swimming in a thickening fog.

The room tilted. The corners of her vision flickered like dying flames. She saw the ceiling spin above her, the lamplight bending and swaying like a ship at sea. Her knees buckled, a marionette's strings cut all at once, and she sank toward the floor.

But just before the world surrendered her to the dark—She saw it.

A glint. Steel, rising. Gleaming. A knife. The blade caught the lamplight one final time, refracting it into a cruel, beautiful gleam—a terrible promise etched in silver. Then it came down, with swift, merciless certainty.

And the room fell silent.

Outside, the grand finale had flared across the heavens in a final act of unrestrained brilliance. Crimson ribbons tore through the sky, chased by gold and silver sparks that danced like embers in a divine forge. A final, thunderous burst split the

142

night in two, echoing across the rooftops with bone-deep resonance. The heavens lit up one last time in a cascading waterfall of glittering light — liquid stars pouring downward in slow, radiant collapse. Gasps rose from the crowd, wide-eyed and breathless, as if the sky itself had wept beauty.

Then, at last, came silence.

A collective pause. The hush that followed something too beautiful to be spoken over. And then — applause. Rolling and joyous, full of praise, awe, and the kind of pure, untainted wonder that only a sky ablaze can conjure. Children clapped with sticky palms, couples exchanged bright-eyed glances, and for one suspended moment, the world belonged to joy alone.

Reverend Meadows came jogging up the path, his breath catching with every step, a flushed grin lighting up his usually solemn features. The collar of his coat fluttered behind him like a forgotten sermon in the wind.

"Don't tell me I've missed it!" he called, breathless but beaming, his voice warm and buoyant with shared delight.

George turned toward him, laughter already dancing on his lips. "I'm afraid so. Now that was a show!" he said, clapping his hands together in open-hearted applause, as if the sky might hear and offer an encore.

"It sure was!" Sarah chimed in, her cheeks aglow with color, eyes still reflecting the molten silver of the finale, as if fragments of the fireworks had settled in her gaze.

"Most definitely!" Reverend Meadows said with a huffing chuckle, brushing at the sleeves of his coat with a theatrical flourish, as though ridding himself of imaginary soot — or perhaps some lingering weight the night had momentarily lifted.

"Let's all go inside, shall we?" Mabel's voice floated above the laughter, smooth and melodic, touched with the gentle cadence of practiced hospitality. She turned toward the house with the easy grace of someone used to welcoming joy across her threshold, her smile serene, her heart content.

She did not know. Not yet.

One by one, they followed — Sarah looping her arm through George's, Reverend Meadows falling into step behind them, the conversation flowing like a gentle current. Their laughter lilted through the night air, a trail of candlelight trailing behind them, casting a fragile glow in the darkness.

But inside the Brown home, that light was already failing.

Beneath the roof they approached so cheerfully, the night had turned. The shadow they were about to step into had teeth, and the silence that awaited them was not that of wonder—but aftermath. What had unfolded behind those walls was no celebration. It was a reckoning, coiled in the quiet, waiting to be found.

And as they crossed the threshold, unaware, their warmth and levity brushed up against a darkness that had already begun to seep through the cracks—silent, patient, and irreversible.

Inside, the Brown home still glimmered with the aftertaste of celebration. The warm light of gas sconces painted the walls in hues of amber and gold, casting soft, flickering shadows that waltzed across the polished floors. The faint scent of cinnamon, mulled wine, and distant smoke still hung in the air, mingling with the residual murmur of laughter from the porch. It felt, for a moment, like the house was still alive with joy. Still breathing.

Marion and Jack lingered near the entryway, caught between the echo of festivities and the pull of something quieter. Something heavier. Jack paused just beneath the transom window, his face tilted skyward as the last of the fireworks stuttered out above them—tiny, final sparks swallowed by the night like stars burning out in a dying universe.

"That was spectacular, wasn't it?" he said softly, the wonder still coloring his voice, though fainter now, as if already retreating into memory.

"It really was," Marion replied, her words barely more than a breath. Her hands rested gently in front of her, fingers laced as though in prayer—or perhaps in preparation.

Jack lowered his gaze, the glow in his expression dimming just slightly. "I still don't understand why Winston and Mabel went through with this party. After everything that's been in the papers... after what this city's become at night."

Marion's smile flickered at the corners of her lips, but her eyes held something quieter. Older. A sorrow wrapped in understanding. "I asked Mabel about it during dinner," she said at last. "She told me it wasn't their idea. It was Abigail's."

Jack blinked. "Abigail?" The name left his lips like a question, like a puzzle piece that didn't quite fit the picture.

"She insisted," Marion said gently. "Said we can't let fear make our choices for us. That if we live in fear, we hand the killer exactly what he wants. She said that even now — especially now — we should live fully." Her voice softened. "She's a remarkable young woman."

Jack gave a slow, quiet nod. "She certainly is." The words landed like a quiet reverence — half admiration, half ache.

And then silence.

Not the empty kind, but the kind that breathes. That listens.

They stepped fully into the foyer, the front door closing behind them with a whisper-soft thud, shutting out the night. Somewhere, deeper in the house, a hallway clock ticked on — a quiet

147

metronome of indifference, carving out seconds in perfect rhythm, oblivious to what those seconds now measured.

Neither of them knew—not yet—that Abigail's courage had met a darkness beyond philosophy or resolve. A darkness with hands. With breath. With eyes that did not blink. Her defiance had not faltered, but even defiance could be silenced. And it had been—utterly, violently, completely. Her final moments had been stolen not just from her, but from the world. No cries. No witness. Just a breath held too long… and then no more breath at all.

The house still wore its celebration like a mask, but beneath it—beneath the glow, beneath the laughter that still lingered faintly in its walls—a terrible stillness waited. A secret crouched in the dark. A scene set and left to be found.

The parlor pulsed with the quiet rhythm of a party winding down. Conversation hummed gently beneath the soft hiss of the hearth, where flames whispered secrets into the stone. Shadows danced along the walls, flickering behind the frames of old portraits and along the edges of polished wainscoting, giving the illusion of movement where there was none. A draft moved through the room like a ghost, brushing against hemlines and sleeve cuffs — noticed, perhaps, but not minded.

Near the sideboard, Matthew stood apart, turning his glass slowly in his hand. The amber drink inside caught the firelight, casting fractured reflections across his knuckles. But his eyes were distant, somewhere far from the warmth of the room. Beside him, Albert watched the fire, his gaze fixed and unblinking, as though trying to divine answers in the shifting coals.

And then there was Uriah — smiling, buoyant, slicing through the lull with his usual irrepressible charm.

"Sounds like everything went off with a smash!" he said, nudging Albert with an elbow and sending a grin toward Matthew.

From the center of the room, Winston answered with a genial laugh. "Oh, it did! You should've seen poor Henry down the street — leapt three feet in the air when the last one popped. I thought he'd lost a year of his life!"

Laughter rolled through the group, a warm tide of release. It softened the walls again, blurred

149

the edges of earlier worries, and made the house feel — for just a moment — like a haven.

"I'll go and fetch Abigail," Mabel said gently, smoothing back a curl with fingers made graceful by habit. Her voice held the practiced cadence of care. "She stepped into the library before the fireworks."

"All right, dear," Winston said, his smile holding, though his eyes followed her a little too long. Something flickered there — concern, perhaps, or just intuition.

Mabel left quietly. Her heels ticked down the hall in steady rhythm, a soft metronome counting down seconds no one else knew were precious.

Across the room, George and Sarah approached. The end of the night hung on their shoulders like a coat too heavy. Sarah tugged her shawl tighter; George offered his hand to Winston.

"We're grateful, truly," George said. "But it's gettin' late, and we've got an early train."

Winston clasped the offered hand with both of his, warm and sincere. "The pleasure was ours. Abigail was especially glad you could make it."

They exchanged goodbyes with nods and soft smiles. And then they turned for the door—just as another moment was beginning to unravel behind them.

At the window, Matthew had leaned toward Mary and Jim, interrupting their quiet conversation. Uriah, ever the opportunist, caught the movement.

"And what about you two?" he called with a grin. "Still game for cards? I hear college kids thrive in moonlight."

Matthew smirked, falling easily into the tease. "They're used to sleepless nights. I imagine they'll wipe the floor with us."

Laughter again. Easy. Familiar.

Until it wasn't.

Jim's smile faltered, then fell. Something steeled in his expression as he leaned back and crossed his arms with finality.

"That's rich," he said, his voice edged. "Coming from a college dropout."

The air changed.

151

It didn't shift—it snapped. Like a wire pulled too tight.

Matthew rose, slow and deliberate. The smile vanished from his face as if wiped clean, replaced by something colder. He straightened to his full height, and it was suddenly too much.

"What did you just say?" he asked, voice low and flat, a warning wrapped in velvet.

All sound drained from the room. Even the fire seemed to quiet. Glasses paused in the air. Conversations stilled mid-word. The room's warmth became fragile— balancing on a single breath.

And then—

A scream. It shattered everything. Ragged. Piercing. Human. It erupted from the depths of the house like something torn from the earth. Not a scream of fright, but of devastation. The kind that gutted the soul.

No one moved.

For a heartbeat—maybe two—the entire world held still.

Then the room exploded into motion. Chairs scraped violently across the floor. Urgent voices collided. People turned, stumbled, ran. George and Sarah wheeled back from the doorway, their departure forgotten. Winston was already moving, color gone from his face, heart beating ahead of his feet. Marion grabbed Jack's arm. Uriah was the first to vanish into the hallway, the smile wiped from his face, replaced by something raw and stricken.

No one asked who had screamed. They didn't need to.

Every soul in the room knew — deep in the marrow, in the part of the human heart that recognizes tragedy before thought can catch up.

And whatever had just been found in the library… it had changed everything.

The doors to the library flew open with a reverberating crash, and the hush that followed felt like the house itself holding its breath.

Mabel was on her knees beneath the looming bookshelves and the cold shimmer of the chandelier. Her shoulders shook with sobs that racked her small frame, raw and untamed, the sound of a woman torn loose from the world she knew. Tears streamed in steady lines down her cheeks, but it was the sound — that second, sharper cry — that shattered the room's composure. It wasn't simply grief. It was anguish, elemental and wild, ripping from her throat as though her body could no longer contain it.

Winston pushed past the stunned cluster of guests, not even aware of the bodies he brushed aside. He dropped to the floor beside her, his arms instinctively wrapping around her, grounding her, but his eyes — his eyes had already locked on the sight across the room.

Abigail.

Her body lay half-concealed behind the sofa, as though the furniture had taken it upon itself to shield her from full view. Only the hem of her dress, artfully fanned out like the petals of a wilted flower, and the limp curve of her bare foot peeked into the light. The angle of her legs told more than any scream could. Something in that stillness — unnatural, untouched — screamed of finality.

Winston didn't move. He didn't speak. The air around him thickened, pressing in.

"Oh my God," Marion gasped behind him, the words almost inaudible as her hand flew to her mouth. Jack reached her just in time, pulling her into his arms before she could see too much. She turned into his chest and trembled, her whole body recoiling from the horror hanging in the room like smoke.

The others remained frozen. No one could look away. And yet, no one dared to speak. It was as though time itself had fractured, each person left to fall through their own stunned silence. Shock drifted through the library like fog, curling into corners and between the spines of books that had watched generations come and go — but never this.

CHAPTER 9

JACK

Time had moved forward, yes—but only in the technical sense. It hadn't flowed or flown; it hadn't soothed or numbed. It had crawled across the floor of the world like a wounded creature dragging itself over broken glass, each second arriving with a sting and leaving behind a fresh, silent wound. The evening had fallen like a shroud over the house, and with it came the sort of quiet that doesn't invite peace but announces the arrival of something unspoken, something irreversible.

The parlor, once the heart of the home, had become a mausoleum of memory. Once vibrant with warmth, with music echoing off its wallpapered walls and laughter hanging in the air like perfume, it now stood in mournful stillness. The fire in the hearth burned, yes — but not as a balm. It burned because it didn't know how not to. Its flicker danced against the ornate wooden panels with no warmth to offer, only a mockery of the life that once pulsed through this room. The light cast long, swaying shadows that moved like ghosts on the walls, and the silence grew thicker with every crackle of flame — an oppressive stillness that seemed to press down on each chest, that turned every breath into an effort.

Winston paced in front of the fire like a man caged by his own mind, like someone trying to outwalk the storm building inside his bones. His steps were stiff and uneven, his arms crossed one moment and hanging the next. His jaw clenched and unclenched without him noticing, the veins in his temples subtly visible under the strain. The skin around his eyes had tightened, drawing the sorrow inward until it sat like stone behind his gaze. He looked like a man searching for something to break simply because it would match the fracture within himself. But there was nothing in that room fragile enough to break that hadn't already broken.

Mabel, small and almost spectral in her grief, sat hunched on the edge of the sofa. She was flanked by Sarah and Marion, though neither dared touch her. There was something in her silence that repelled comfort, something in the glassy stare of her swollen eyes that said she had journeyed somewhere far beyond the parlor and could not yet find her way back. Her hands were clenched so tightly in her lap that the knuckles had turned the color of bone. And they trembled — trembled with the sorrow she had no words for, trembled with the effort it took to keep from wailing aloud. She stared not at the fire, nor at the others, but into the invisible space where Abigail had once stood.

Across the room, near the hearth, Reverend Meadows sat hunched forward, elbows resting on his knees, hands clasped before him as though in prayer. He spoke in the tone of a man who had stood in too many rooms like this one, who had seen grief wear too many faces and never once found the right words. His voice was low, steady, gently insistent — a sound that tried to anchor the room.

"Winston, my friend," he said quietly, leaning just slightly forward, "I am so sorry for your loss. Abigail was... she was a light in this home. Even I, just a visitor now and then, could feel it."

Winston didn't answer. He kept his back turned to them, his eyes locked onto something beyond the parlor window. Outside, the night had thickened into an ink-black void, the stars absent, the moon a ghost behind clouded veils. He said nothing for a long moment, until finally his voice emerged — cracked, brittle, as though dragged up from a dry well.

"Where are they?" he asked, still not turning.

Jack, who had remained standing near the mantle in an uneasy stillness, unfolded his arms and stepped forward slightly, voice careful and measured. "They'll be here soon, Winston. Just a little longer. Don't worry."

That turned Winston's head. His gaze landed on Jack with a sharpness that cut. There was no gratitude in it, no trust — only the suspicion of a man who had lost too much to believe in reassurances.

"With these men," Winston said, his tone flat and bitter, "I'm not so sure anymore."

159

His words fell into the room like a stone into still water, sending ripples through the silence. No one replied. No one moved. They knew better.

And then, as though summoned by that doubt — by the weight of it pressing against the walls of the house — the doorbell rang.

It was not a gentle chime. It was a low, resonant note that cleaved through the hush like a knife through skin. The parlor stiffened. The sound lingered in the air long after it had faded, vibrating somewhere deep in each chest. Even the fire seemed to pause in its crackle.

Winston's head snapped toward the hallway. Before anyone could speak, before a single foot lifted from the floor, he was already moving. He strode out of the room with the weight of finality in his steps, urgency wrapped tight around every muscle. Jack followed behind him without a word, and Reverend Meadows stood, sighing softly before trailing them as well.

Back in the parlor, no one else moved. The stillness that followed their departure was not calm. It was full of tension, as though the room itself held its breath. The women sat locked in place, staring at the hallway beyond which

160

Winston had vanished, staring into the unknowable.

And in that moment — though no one spoke it aloud — they all understood something fundamental had shifted. The sound of that bell, the approaching echo of boots, the weight in Winston's footsteps — none of it was ordinary. Something had arrived with the night, something beyond grief or explanation. A line had been crossed. A veil had lifted. And whatever waited on the other side of that door — whoever it was, whatever it brought — would change everything.

Nothing in the Brown household would ever be the same again.

The heavy front door creaked open, its hinges groaning in protest as the night spilled into the house like a breath long held. The air that rushed in was cold and damp, soaked in the scent of wet earth and withering leaves, wrapping around the threshold like a warning. Outside, beneath the shelter of the portico, two figures stood side by side — the yellow glow from the porch lamp above casting their shadows long and uneven across the checkered floor. For a moment, no one spoke. The silence pressed down with the weight of the dead.

The first to break it was the younger man. "Good evening, Mr. Brown," he said gently, his voice touched with a soft Southern drawl — not exaggerated, but natural, melodic, and strangely out of place in the grand, solemn house before him. He removed his hat respectfully, holding it close to his chest. Detective Clark Baxter had the kind of face that might have once belonged to a boy raised in sun-drenched fields — neat blond hair, fair skin, clean-shaven and open. But his eyes betrayed more than youth. They were cautious, intelligent, quietly searching — as if already trying to piece together what had been broken here before even stepping inside.

Beside him stood a man who couldn't have been more different — taller, broader, older, with a wide frame that blocked part of the light. Detective Fred Bryant looked as though he'd been carved from stone left too long in the rain — graying hair, sun-darkened skin, and a mouth that rarely curled into anything other than a sneer. He did not wait for invitation or instruction. He simply stepped inside, boots heavy on the floor, coat still damp from the mist. The way he moved — slow, deliberate — was less about reverence and more about ownership, like

162

a man walking into a place he already didn't respect.

Detective Bryant's eyes swept over the interior with the idle arrogance of someone who'd already decided what he thought. He took in the details — the smooth, polished wood beneath his feet, the gilded picture frames along the wall, the delicate chandelier hanging above like a relic from a forgotten century. He gave a low whistle, not out of admiration but mockery, the sound whistling between his teeth like wind through broken glass.

"So," he said, stretching the syllable lazily, "this is what the inside of it looks like?" His lips twisted in a half-smile that held no warmth. "Even got electricity. Fancy. It's alright, I suppose."

The words hung in the air like smoke, souring the space around them. Winston Brown stiffened where he stood. The muscles along his jaw pulsed. His hand, still resting against the doorframe, curled slightly. A retort began to form on his lips, something bitter, something earned — but before it could surface, Jack gently reached out and caught his arm, offering only a glance.

The look was subtle, but strong: Don't. Not now. Not with him.

Detective Baxter, still lingering at the threshold, looked mortified. His eyes darted to his partner, then back to Winston, apology flickering faintly across his features. He had the decency to look ashamed — for the man he arrived with, for the tone that had infected the room, for the stain it left on a night already bloodied by grief. "May we come in, Mr. Brown?" he asked quietly, his voice almost reverent now. "I'm truly sorry... for your loss."

Winston, though still bristling, managed a small nod. "Come in," he said hoarsely, his voice rough from grief and restraint.

Detective Baxter stepped in like a man entering sacred ground, his movements careful, his eyes already scanning the room not for evidence, but for emotional residue — the kind of intangible heaviness left behind after something terrible happens. Meanwhile, Detective Bryant snorted under his breath and muttered to Detective Baxter with no attempt to keep the words private.

"Why're you bein' so polite? Ain't like they're supposed to care."

The insult was casual, thoughtless — but in a room this raw, it was like a slap. Every sound seemed to fall away in the moments that followed. No one spoke. No one moved.

Detective Bryant turned his head slowly and eyed the three men in the hallway — Winston, Jack, and Reverend Meadows — with a look of vague disinterest, as though evaluating livestock before a sale. When his gaze landed on Reverend Meadows and the white collar peeking from beneath his coat, he actually scoffed, as if the presence of a man of God made the scene more comical than sacred. Then, as though bored by the silence, he cut straight to the bone.

"Where's the body?"

There was no emotion in the question. No hesitation. Just the blunt reality, thrown down like a gauntlet. It landed hard.

Winston didn't answer. He looked at Detective Bryant — really looked at him — and something deep and bitter passed behind his eyes. Then, slowly, with hands that trembled only slightly, he reached behind him and closed the front door with a firm, deliberate push. The latch clicked shut, and the sound echoed through the vast, hollow house like a final verdict. For a brief

165

second, his hand stayed on the knob, his fingers tight, as if he were holding back the floodwaters of his grief by sheer will.

Without a word, he turned and began walking down the hall.

Detective Baxter followed close behind, his head slightly bowed, hat still in hand. Detective Bryant followed too, slower, his steps echoing like an afterthought. Jack and Reverend Meadows exchanged a glance — one filled with quiet, simmering rage — then fell into step at the rear. The hallway stretched out before them like a tunnel into something unspeakable. Each footstep on the old floorboards creaked louder than the last.

The house had changed. It was no longer a place of laughter, or celebration, or memory. It was something else now. Something hollowed. A stage upon which grief performed its cruelest soliloquy.

And at the end of that hallway, behind those towering shelves and the flickering chandelier, the truth — whatever shape it would take — waited in the library, cloaked in shadows and silence.

The air in the library was thick with sorrow and tension. A single lamp burned dimly in the corner, casting a faint, golden glow across the hardwood floors and polished shelves that lined the room like silent sentinels. In the center of the room, Abigail's lifeless form lay still, a stark and terrible contrast against the elegance of her surroundings.

Winston Brown stepped through the doorway, his shoulders squared, but his eyes betrayed him. They flicked toward his daughter's body, then away just as quickly — as though even a second of contact might destroy what was left of his composure.

"She's here," he said quietly, his voice brittle.

Detectives Bryant and Baxter entered behind him. Bryant strode in first, his demeanor unbothered and brash, as if he were stepping into a barn rather than a crime scene. He surveyed the room with little emotion, his eyes settling briefly on the body before turning to the others.

"And you're certain you found her like this?" he asked, his tone accusatory.

Jack, standing just off to the side, nodded firmly.

"That's right, sir."

Detective Bryant tilted his head toward the reverend. "And no one else was in the room with her?"

"We're positive," Reverend Meadows answered, steady but weary.

Detective Bryant scoffed, his lip curling. He fixed the reverend with a slow, scrutinizing glare, letting the silence stretch before sneering.

"Are you sure?" he said, his voice now laced with venom. "Look, it's the Fourth of July. Just admit it — one of you in this house got a little drunk. Things got awry and, all of a sudden, the girl is dead."

Jack's mouth fell open. "What? That's not what happened! We just told you—"

Bryant cut him off with a wave of his hand. "And I'm just supposed to take your word for it? Please. I know how you people get sometimes. You just—"

"Fred, for Christ's sake!" Detective Baxter snapped, clearly mortified.

Winston stepped forward sharply, rage bubbling to the surface. "Are you saying I don't know my own mind, you—"

Detective Bryant squared up to him, a cruel smile touching the corners of his mouth. "You better be careful," he said coldly. "Just 'cause you live in this fancy house... don't mean it can protect you."

"Is that a threat?" Winston's voice was a low growl.

Detective Bryant leaned in, their faces inches apart. "Call it a warning...boy."

The word landed like a slap, and the two men stood toe to toe, neither flinching. Jack and Reverend Meadows moved instinctively, hands twitching at their sides, uncertain whether to intervene.

Eventually, Bryant broke the silence. Without shifting his stance, he spoke to Baxter. "Leave the girl here."

The words struck Winston like a fresh blow.

All three men — Winston, Jack, and Reverend Meadows — cried out in objection.

Detective Bryant spun around. "Look! There's nothing we can do. This is officially a crime scene. We'll leave her here until the morning. We've already got eight other bodies stacked up thanks to this so-called 'Ripper.'" He glanced back at Abigail's form. "Looks like your girl just became the ninth."

Winston's fists clenched. "She was not my girl," he said, voice trembling. Then, more quietly, almost broken, "She was my daughter."

His grief cracked the veneer of control he had so fiercely held. Jack and Reverend Meadows both stepped closer, placing comforting hands on his back. The gesture grounded him, but the pain in his eyes was unmistakable.

Detective Baxter's jaw tightened. He was clearly affected, but Detective Bryant remained unmoved — cold and detached.

"Well, like I said," Bryant muttered. "Nothin' we can do. We'll just have to wait 'til the mornin'."

Winston lifted his chin defiantly, forcing himself upright. He would not fall apart in front of a man so heartless.

Detective Baxter, looking pale, shifted uncomfortably. "Fred, we can't just leave her like this. We can at least... cover the young lady. Surely?"

Bryant turned, giving his partner a dismissive glance.

"Lady?" he scoffed.

Then, looking back at the body, he muttered, "Sure.

Do what you want."

He paused, eyes flicking toward Reverend Meadows again. "Look at you," he sneered. "Mingling with the likes of them..."

He shook his head, the word that followed oozing with disdain.

"...Traitor."

Without waiting for a response, Detective Bryant turned and left the library. Moments later, the sound of the front door slamming echoed through the house like a gunshot.

Detective Baxter remained, awkward and ashamed. "I do apologize for my partner. He can be..."

"An asshole?" Reverend Meadows said flatly. "Reverend!" Jack gasped, turning toward him.

The reverend gave a wry, bitter smile. "Even I can have a slip now and then, Mr. Franklin. And in this case, I think it's warranted."

Jack turned his glare toward Baxter now. "And you sure stood up to him real firm while he was saying all those terrible things, didn't you?"

Baxter flinched. "I know. And I do apologize. Truly. He makes things for me at the station a nightmare as it is. But believe me when I say — there really is nothing we can do until morning. This room is a crime scene now."

Winston, disillusioned and disgusted, turned sharply on his heel and left the room. Reverend Meadows followed close behind, his robes swishing as he disappeared down the hall.

Jack remained with the younger detective, arms crossed tightly. "Look, you seem like a decent guy. Are you sure there's nothing that can be done?"

"I'm sure, Mr...?" "Franklin."

"Mr. Franklin," Baxter repeated. "There's nothing the police can do here tonight. We have to wait on the coroner, and he won't be available until morning."

He paused for a moment, thinking. Then his eyes narrowed.

"There aren't many people in this house, are there?

She was found here alone?"

Jack nodded. "That's right. We'd just finished watching fireworks. Everyone went outside."

"Everyone?" "I believe so."

Baxter exhaled slowly, nodding to himself. "Alright. I'm going to have a look around — check for signs of a break-in. Somebody might've slipped in while everyone was distracted. I'll go find Mr. Brown so he can accompany me."

He began walking toward the door.

"What about your partner?" Jack asked.

Baxter paused at the threshold, then turned back.

"Let him take care of himself. He may not want to do his job — but we took an oath to protect and serve. I intend to do both tonight."

173

A beat passed.

"In the meantime, do you know where they keep the sheets?"

A faint, almost grateful smile broke across Jack's face. Without another word, he turned to find them.

Jack returned to the library, a tightly folded white sheet pressed to his chest like a sacred offering. His face bore the raw etchings of sorrow, every line and contour burdened with a weight too great for words. At the doorway, he hesitated, letting his gaze drift toward Abigail's still form beneath the dim light. We did not see her — only the hollow, aching absence reflected in his eyes.

With quiet reverence, Jack stepped inside. The hush of the room embraced him like a mausoleum, and for a moment he simply stood there, breathing in the grief that clung to the air. Then, wordlessly, he moved forward and knelt beside her. His hands trembled as he unfolded the sheet. There was no urgency in the act — only care, devotion. He laid the fabric gently over her, drawing it up over her shoulders, across her chest, and finally to her face. Each motion was deliberate, performed as though a too-hasty gesture might desecrate what little dignity the dead still possessed.

Once finished, Jack remained kneeling beside her, his fingertips lingering on the smooth linen for a breath too long. His head bowed. A whisper of silence passed between them — the living and the lost. Then, quietly, he rose and walked away.

CHAPTER 10

MARION

The footsteps came slowly, echoing faintly in the cavernous space of the Brown residence. Winston Brown descended first, his figure tall but bent slightly forward, like a man too burdened to stand entirely upright. Behind him, Detective Baxter followed, a silent sentinel cloaked in the kind of fatigue reserved only for men who carry too many unanswered questions. Their shadows spilled across the marbled floor in long, stretched forms — elongated specters cast by the dim, yellow glow of the antique chandelier that hung overhead like a ghost from a more dignified past.

The foyer, once a place of cheerful arrivals and warm goodnights, had taken on the somber chill of a mausoleum. The grand staircase, with its polished banisters and runner rug worn thin by generations of Brown family footsteps, no longer felt like a gateway to bedrooms and nursery rooms — it now loomed like a passageway into grief itself. Every corner of the house seemed to retreat into itself, shrinking beneath the weight of the tragedy that had unfolded under its roof. The silence was profound, oppressive, almost sacred. It clung to the walls like mist, thick and watchful.

At the bottom of the stairs, Jack Franklin waited, his frame rigid with tension. His arms were folded tightly across his chest, his shoulders stiff with the effort of holding himself together. A muscle jumped in his jaw, working against the restraint he was forcing on himself. His eyes moved between the two men descending toward him — one his friend, broken and drowning in sorrow, and the other a stranger cloaked in the authority of justice but trailing shadows of helplessness behind him.

177

When they reached the final step, Baxter spoke. He cleared his throat first, but the sound was barely more than a breath — a concession to formality in a house where formalities had become meaningless.

"I've completed the preliminary search," he said, his voice careful, measured, as if volume alone might disturb the dead. "Every room, every hallway, upstairs and down. I've checked the locks, the latches, the windowsills, the cellar door, even the chimney flue."

His words hovered in the still air for a moment before he continued.

"There's no evidence of forced entry. Nothing broken. No tool marks. No scratches on locks or hinges. No muddy footprints. No scuffed floors that don't belong.

No sign — not a single one — of anyone having entered from the outside."

He turned his head slightly to face Winston, whose eyes were unfocused, staring at some fixed point in the distant dark beyond the front door.

"I'm sorry," Baxter said, more gently now. "I can't yet tell you how this happened... but I promise you, I will find out who did this."

Winston blinked, slowly, and for a brief moment seemed to return from the hollow place where his mind had been wandering. His voice, when it came, was so quiet it nearly vanished into the hush of the house.

"Your honesty... is appreciated, Detective. It's more than we've had from others. Thank you."

And with that, Winston turned. Not abruptly, but as if every muscle in his body required negotiation before it could obey. His shoulders were bowed beneath the invisible weight of the loss he carried, and each step he took across the foyer floor was that of a man trudging through grief made manifest — thick as water, heavy as stone.

Baxter watched him go in silence, his own expression dark with sympathy that had nowhere to land. Then, after a moment, he shifted his attention back to Jack, whose eyes were still burning with questions.

"Mr. Franklin," Baxter began, lowering his voice to a near whisper as he stepped closer, "earlier this evening, you asked if there was something useful you could do."

Jack nodded, quickly, the response instinctive and laced with urgency. "Yes. Anything. Just tell me what you need."

The detective glanced briefly down the hallway, where the flickering light from the parlor cast soft shadows. His jaw tightened before he spoke.

"I've been thinking about something you said earlier," he began slowly. "You mentioned that during the fireworks, the entire household had stepped outside. That everyone had gone out to the lawn."

Jack nodded again, but this time with less certainty. "Yes...yes, that's right. We'd finished dinner, and everyone was excited. Everyone went to watch."

Baxter's gaze grew darker.

"I don't think that's the full truth."

The words landed hard. Jack frowned, confused, defensive. "What are you saying?"

"There's no forced entry," Detective Baxter replied, voice steady but grave. "No broken doors. No unlocked windows. Nothing to indicate an intruder ever came into this house from the outside."

Jack blinked, the implication sinking in with all the subtlety of a dagger.

"You're not suggesting..." he began, but his voice faltered.

"I am," Baxter said, finishing it for him. "I believe someone was already here. Inside. When it happened. Someone who belonged."

Jack's blood ran cold. He felt it drain from his face, leaving behind only a mix of shock and horror. "You mean...one of us?"

The detective didn't respond immediately, but his silence was answer enough.

Jack took a step back. "Are you saying that the person who killed Abigail is in this house...right now?"

"I do," Detective Baxter said quietly. "I don't know who. Not yet. But the evidence points inward. And until we know more, we need to be cautious."

The silence that followed was immense. Jack's hands curled into fists, knuckles whitening.

181

"Then why aren't you doing anything?" he demanded, his voice rising with disbelief. "Why aren't you arresting someone? Why are you just standing there?"

"Because we can't," Baxter answered, the frustration raw in his own voice now. "Not without proof. Not without cause. I know how this looks, but we have to follow the law, Jack. Even when it hurts."

"Don't you dare ask me to be patient," Jack snapped, voice sharp with grief-fueled rage. "That girl — that sweet, innocent girl — is dead in the next room, and you're standing here talking about procedures?"

"I'm not asking for patience," Baxter said, hands raised slightly, not in surrender but in appeal. "I'm asking for caution. Because if the killer is still here, then they're watching. Listening. Waiting. And the wrong move could send them running — or worse, make them strike again."

"If the police won't do anything about that poor girl in there," said Jack, "then we'll figure out who did it on our own."

Detective Baxter knew there was no way convincing him. Jack's breath came fast, his body trembling with the force of his anger. Then, without another word, he turned on his heel and strode off down the hallway, his footfalls heavy and urgent. The parlor swallowed him, and with him, the last of the foyer's fragile calm.

Baxter stood alone, the vast silence settling once again like dust after a collapse. He didn't follow. He couldn't. Instead, he remained rooted, shoulders stiff, eyes locked on the dark corridor ahead.

And slowly, his chest rose and fell with a breath that was more sigh than exhale — a breath drawn not to steady himself, but to keep from collapsing beneath the helplessness that clung to him like a second skin.

Detective Baxter lingered just beyond the threshold of the parlor, his hat resting solemnly in one hand. The light from the wall sconces bathed his silhouette in a warm gold, softening the weary angles of his face. Though his posture was composed, his eyes betrayed the burden of what he carried — the weight of loss he'd seen too many times before.

"Mr. and Mrs. Brown," he said gently, his voice carrying the lilt of a Southern drawl, quiet but firm, "I'll leave you now. I just want you to know how sorry I am for your loss. And that I'll be prayin' for you and your family."

The words, simple and unpolished, settled over the room like a blanket. They cut through the fog of grief not with grandeur but with grace — unexpected, intimate. Something in them found Mabel. Despite the tears sliding freely down her cheeks, she lifted her eyes and gave a faint, trembling smile.

"Thank you," she whispered, voice hollowed by sorrow but touched by gratitude.

Detective Baxter nodded once, respectfully, then placed his hat back on his head with the kind of care one gives to small, sacred things. He turned and walked down the hallway, the heels of his shoes muffled against the polished floor. Moments later, the soft click of the front door closing reverberated faintly through the house — quiet, final, and irrevocably solemn.

Jack remained apart from the others, leaning against the wall, arms folded tight against his chest. He was still — too still — and the storm in his eyes only grew darker. His gaze found

Marion, seated beside Mabel, gently dabbing her friend's tears with a folded handkerchief. She looked up, sensing his stare.

"Marion," he said, his voice low and measured.

She blinked and turned toward him, her own grief softened only by empathy. "Yes?"

"May I speak with you for a moment?"

Marion glanced briefly at Mabel, offered a reassuring squeeze of her hand, and rose without question. "Of course."

Together, they stepped silently out of the parlor. Their footsteps were faint against the hardwood floor, almost respectful, like even sound itself dared not disturb the fragile air of mourning.

CHAPTER 11

JACK

The dining room, untouched by tragedy, seemed frozen in time. The long table stretched beneath a crystal chandelier, its linen pristine, the silverware perfectly aligned. A tall vase of lilies — fresh, pale, fragrant — stood in the center, their innocence now almost jarring in contrast to the storm gathering outside the room.

Jack told her everything — what he'd seen, what Baxter had said. About the theory that chilled him to the bone: Abigail hadn't been killed by someone who broke in. No locks had been tampered with. No windows forced. No footprints tracked in from the outside.

Whoever had done it…had never left.

Marion stood in stunned silence, arms folded, her expression slowly shifting from disbelief to dawning dread.

"That's unbelievable," she whispered, her voice nearly lost in the cavernous quiet of the room.

Jack stepped closer. "That's why I need your help. I can't do this on my own. And let's be honest — you're the brains in this relationship."

A corner of her mouth lifted in the shadow of a smile.

"Well, that is true."

But the moment passed quickly. The mirth fell away like a mask.

"Oh, Jack…" she murmured, her voice cracking under the weight of it. "We shouldn't joke. Not now. That poor girl… Abigail… she was just a child."

He looked away, jaw tightening. "And the cops? They've got nothing. Just speculation. She was killed the same way the others were. Ripper-style. But here — in this house. And that means..."

He trailed off. He didn't need to finish.

Marion went pale. "It means the killer is still here."

Jack gave a slow nod.

Silence stretched between them, tense and electric. Then Marion drew in a breath and straightened, setting her shoulders with quiet resolve.

"Well," she said, clear and certain, "if you think we can help... then help we shall."

Jack looked at her, something new flickering in his eyes — hope. A fragile hope, maybe, but hope nonetheless.

"What are we going to do?" he asked.

Marion was already thinking, her expression sharpening.

"I think I have a plan," she said simply. Then she turned and walked toward the door with unhurried confidence, the kind that spoke of purpose.

Jack didn't hesitate. He followed her into the darkened hallway, the silence between them now filled not with fear, but with quiet determination.

The room remained suspended in an oppressive, unnatural stillness — the kind that settles only after joy has been ripped violently from its roots. The fire in the hearth still glowed, but no one drew warmth from it anymore. Instead, grief clung to the walls like soot, seeping into the wallpaper, hanging in the curtains, coiling between the floorboards like an invisible smoke.

No one had moved in some time. They merely existed now — fragments of a once-celebratory evening, trapped in a tableau of shock.

Marion moved slowly across the parlor, her steps so light they barely made a sound, as if she feared disturbing the dead. The fabric of her dress whispered against the floor, the soft swish mournful, almost funereal. She crossed to the fireplace where Reverend Meadows stood, deep in hushed conversation with Winston, who had aged ten years in an hour.

"Reverend," Marion said, her voice low but firm — like a note played on a cello in a silent chapel — "may we see you for a moment?"

The Reverend turned toward her, the deep lines in his face shadowed by firelight. His eyes, usually gentle, looked dim now — clouded with fatigue, sorrow, and the heavy burden of helplessness.

"Certainly," he replied, his voice worn and thinned, as though every word cost something.

As he stepped away from Winston, George Stevens quietly replaced him, a steadying hand placed on his shoulder. The two men spoke in tones too low to catch, but his grief was visible — pressing down on him like stone.

Marion waited until the Reverend was beside her before leaning in, her voice just above a whisper, but sharp with something deliberate beneath the surface.

"This whole situation is just... so tragic, isn't it?"

Reverend Meadows sighed, the sound drawn from somewhere deep in his chest. "Absolutely terrible," he murmured. "That poor young woman." He shook his head slowly, heavily. "I pray they find the monster who did this — and soon."

Marion's lips parted, but she hesitated — as though weighing each word like glass. Then she tilted her head, almost gently, and said, "Perhaps we should talk in the dining room?"

The Reverend blinked, surprised by the sudden shift.

"What?" he asked, uncertain.

"It'll only take a moment," she repeated, softer this time, though her tone had not lost its edge of quiet urgency.

A flicker of doubt passed through his eyes — just a flash — as if his instincts tugged him back, whispered to him that now wasn't the time. But the doubt faded just as quickly. Whatever thoughts he had, he smothered them beneath his collar and gave a slow, reluctant nod.

"Very well."

And so the three of them — Marion, Jack, and Reverend Meadows — stepped out of the parlor. Not in haste. Not in fear. But with the measured stillness of those who know they are walking toward something inevitable.

Behind them, the parlor remained frozen — the air unmoving, the guests adrift in their own shadows.

They left the weight of grief behind them. And walked straight into the quiet jaws of something far heavier. Something waiting.

Marion and Jack led Reverend Meadows into the dining room, and the door clicked shut behind them like a seal. The air inside was different — denser, somehow. Still warm from earlier laughter and candlelight, yet laced now with suspicion and something unspoken... something rotten. The lingering scent of candle wax curled through the room like a ghost, mixing with the acrid edge of fear.

The long mahogany table stood untouched — the polished silverware aligned with mechanical precision, the delicate china gleaming faintly beneath the overhead chandelier. Yet the scene felt abandoned, as though a celebration had been interrupted mid-breath by the arrival of death itself. The table no longer hosted a meal — it bore witness.

Reverend Meadows hovered near the chair at the table's end, his eyes shifting between Marion and Jack with caution. His brow furrowed, jaw tight with restraint.

"Is there something I can help you both with?" he asked, his voice measured, but there was steel beneath it — the kind that comes from knowing you're being cornered.

"Yes, you can," Jack replied, his tone calm, but his gaze didn't waver. It was the kind of look that stripped away masks.

The Reverend didn't respond, but the silence stretched — taut and waiting.

"We'd like to know what you were doing," Jack said, his voice quiet but deliberate, "between the time the fireworks began… and when they ended."

The question didn't fall — it landed. Hard. Like a dropped stone in still water.

The Reverend blinked, slowly. "What do you mean?" he asked, though his tone had gone noticeably cooler.

"I mean," Jack said, "you were the last person to come outside. I saw you. You joined us right as the fireworks were dying out."

Reverend Meadows' eyes narrowed. "Is that a crime, Mr. Franklin?"

"No," Marion replied, her voice as smooth and sharp as broken porcelain. "But it is suspicious. Abigail was murdered during that window of time."

The Reverend's mouth tightened. He looked from one face to the other — searching, measuring. Then he said, carefully, "Forgive me, Mrs. Franklin, but it sounds an awful lot like you and your husband are implying that I had something to do with her death."

"We're not implying anything," Jack said quickly, though the air betrayed him — charged now, brittle. "We're saying the timing doesn't add up."

"There's nothing mysterious about it," Reverend Meadows said stiffly, his voice rising. "I had to use the facilities. That's all."

Marion took a step closer. "Are you certain?"

His eyes flared. "Of course I'm certain. And besides—" He paused, visibly weighing his next words. "I wasn't the only one still inside when it happened."

"We know," Jack said, voice steady. "We'll be speaking with them too."

There was a flicker of something in the Reverend's face — resentment? Panic? It was gone too quickly to name. He exhaled sharply, frustration thick in his voice.

"I may have done a lot of things in my life," he said, "but I am no murderer. I'm a man of God, for goodness' sake."

Marion tilted her head ever so slightly, her voice dropping into something deeper, colder. "Beware of false prophets, which come to you in sheep's clothing, but inwardly they are ravening wolves."

The silence that followed was thunderous. Meadows stared at her, the verse hanging between them like a blade.

"Matthew 7:15," he muttered. His jaw clenched. "I know the scripture, Mrs. Franklin."

He folded his arms tightly. "Look...I stand by what I said. I'm a guest in this house, same as you."

"And that brings us to our next question," Jack said. "How do you know the Browns?"

195

The Reverend's eyes sharpened. "I could ask you the same."

"You could," Jack said. "But I asked first."

A long pause. Then, with a visible breath, Meadows relented. "Very well," he said at last. "I'm an associate of Winston's. We've...worked together before."

"On what?" Marion asked, voice clipped.

The Reverend hesitated — just long enough for the tension to ratchet higher.

"My assignment here in Atlanta. I wasn't just sent here to preach." His voice dropped a register. "I was sent to protect."

Jack frowned. "Protect who?"

Meadows exhaled through his nose, jaw flexing. "I was placed here by the NAACP. My real mission is to help prevent more bloodshed — more retribution from the violence of white mobs in the area, as some might call it. My sermons are a cover. My collar...is armor."

Marion's eyes widened. "At dinner... when you spoke of the massacre back in 1906 — you said you'd have protected your brethren." She stepped forward. "You're one of us, aren't you?"

196

The Reverend met her eyes. There was no longer room for denial.

"I am," he said, solemn. "I've passed in every city I've been assigned to. It's how I survive. It's how I serve."

He sat down slowly, his hands folded now — not in prayer, but in exhaustion. "I told Winston in confidence. Abigail overheard us talking...and I panicked."

Jack leaned forward, voice gentler now. "What did she hear? How did you feel when Abigail overheard your conversation with Winston?" he asked.

"She heard everything," Reverend Meadows responded. "I felt terrible. I entrusted my secret with Winston because I knew he wouldn't tell anyone. I wasn't so sure my secret would be safe with Abigail. It was the look she gave me that made me uncertain. So many lives depend on my true race being kept a secret."

"You'd be exposed," Marion said. "The entire network would be at risk."

"Yes," he admitted, pain curling through the word.

Jack's eyes narrowed. "So, to protect your secret... you silenced her?"

Meadows' hand slammed onto the table, rattling the silverware.

"I didn't kill her!" he barked. His face flushed, breathing ragged. "You think I don't grieve for her? You think I don't wish I could take back that moment, stop her from hearing it? But murder? That is not who I am!"

Jack raised both palms, easing the heat between them.

The Reverend stood slowly, shoulders rigid.

"I hope you find the killer," he said, quieter now. "I truly do. But I will not stand here and be crucified for something I did not do."

He looked between them once more — his expression unreadable, fractured somewhere between sorrow and fury — then turned and left the room.

His footsteps echoed down the long hallway, fading into the hush like a gavel in an empty courtroom. And still, the air in the dining room pulsed with something unresolved.

198

As if the truth had passed through...But hadn't finished speaking.

CHAPTER 12

MARION

The parlor had changed in the hour since Abigail's lifeless body had been discovered, though no furniture had been moved. The air now hung heavier, thickened by a shared grief that dared not speak aloud. The chandelier overhead, once a centerpiece of quiet elegance, now threw long shadows that clawed at the walls and ceiling. Every glint on the silver tray, every whisper of fabric or muffled cough, carried with it a nervous undercurrent. The room was no longer a sanctuary; it was a stage — and everyone inside, a reluctant actor in a tragedy still unfolding.

Mabel sat on the edge of the sofa, hands twisted together in her lap like a rosary of regret. Her eyes — bloodshot and swollen — remained fixed on the empty spot by the window where Abigail had last stood, laughing not long before the world went sideways.

Marion moved to her, lowering herself to the floor beside the grieving woman with a grace that held no pretense, only purpose.

"Mabel," she said, the name shaped gently on her tongue, "is there anything I can bring you? Tea, perhaps? A blanket?"

Mabel shook her head slowly. Her lips trembled with the effort to hold everything in. "No," she whispered. "Thank you. Just... being here. All of you." She glanced briefly toward Sarah, who sat motionless beside her, and offered a small, fractured smile. "That's enough."

Meanwhile, across the parlor, Albert Oliver stood by the grand piano — his tall frame angled toward the keys, but not playing. His fingers hovered just above the ivory, tracing invisible patterns as though he were trying to summon a

201

memory rather than music. His eyes, however, were distant. Watching something no one else could see.

Jack approached quietly. "I'm surprised you're still here, Mr. Oliver."

Albert didn't look at him right away. When he did, the emotion in his face was unreadable — somewhere between guilt, fatigue, and a sort of muted defiance. "I couldn't leave Matthew. Not after this. Not now."

Jack nodded slowly, then added, as if casually, "Actually… I think I dropped something earlier. In the dining room. Would you mind helping me look?"

Albert hesitated. A flicker of something — suspicion, maybe — passed over his features. But then he gave a slow, measured shrug. "Sure."

Jack turned, offering a small smile and stepping aside to clear the path. As Albert passed through the threshold, Marion rose smoothly from her place beside Mabel and followed without a word, like a shadow that had just remembered its body.

From across the room, near the farthest corner cloaked in shadow, Uriah and Matthew sat apart from the others — low-voiced and leaning in close. They had been whispering for several minutes now, their conversation just out of reach, like smoke slipping between fingers.

As Jack, Marion, and Albert disappeared from view, Uriah turned his head ever so slightly, watching their retreat. His eyes locked with Matthew's. No words were exchanged. None were needed.

The glance between them was fleeting but precise — a quicksilver flick of understanding. A silent confession, or maybe a warning. Whichever it was, it cut through the quiet more deeply than any spoken accusation.

Whatever was happening behind the closed doors of this house, it had not yet reached its end.

And in the silence that followed, one thing became clear:

The truth wasn't just waiting to be uncovered. It was hunting.

The room held a heavy stillness, the kind that seemed to absorb sound and breath alike. The only noise to break it was the faint, rhythmic scrape of Albert's cane as it tapped against the aged wooden floor. Each step seemed to echo with an unspoken tension, a reminder of the weight of age, of secrets too long carried. Slowly, he bent down to peer beneath the table, his knees creaking along with the floorboards, his fingers brushing dust as they searched the shadows. He was methodical, deliberate, as though performing the motion out of obligation more than hope. The silence wrapped around him, thick and watchful.

Jack stood nearby, his posture rigid, arms crossed loosely over his chest as his eyes tracked Albert's every movement. His gaze flitted from the floor to Albert's hands, to the corners of the room, searching not just for the lost object they claimed to seek, but for the undercurrent of truth beneath the moment. And yet— nothing. No trinket, no scrap of significance. Just emptiness. And the feeling that something, unseen, was pressing in from all sides.

In the doorway, Marion stood like a sentinel. Her hands were clasped lightly before her, but her presence was anything but passive. Her eyes moved between the two men, calm but alert, absorbing everything with a quiet, pointed awareness. She didn't speak, not yet. She simply waited.

Albert exhaled slowly, the breath long and heavy as he straightened himself up with effort. A faint grimace flickered across his face as he settled his weight back onto his cane. He looked up at Jack, his expression unreadable for a moment, then spoke in a tone that carried the weariness of someone who had lived too long with things unsaid.

"I'm afraid I don't see anything, Mr. Franklin," he murmured, his voice dry, edged with fatigue. He turned slightly and, with a mild start, realized Marion had been standing there the entire time. "Oh—Mrs. Franklin. I didn't see you there."

She smiled at him gently, a softness in her tone that contrasted with the tension in the room. "Don't worry, Albert. It's alright. Will you have a seat, please?"

With a small nod, Albert lowered himself into a nearby chair, the motion slow and deliberate, as if even this simple act bore the burden of age or regret. He rested his cane carefully against his leg and settled back, the silence reforming around them like mist. But this time, it was not the silence of stillness. It was anticipation.

After a long pause, Albert glanced between the two of them. "I suddenly get the feeling," he said, voice tinged with irony, "that I wasn't called in here to look for anything that's lost."

Jack shifted his stance, leaning against the doorframe now, arms folded across his chest like a barrier. "Well," he said, the words slow, deliberate, "that's not entirely true. Something is lost in this house. And my wife and I... we need to find it right away."

Albert's brow arched slightly. "And what is that?"

Marion's answer came softly, but there was no mistaking the steel beneath her words. "The answer to who killed Abigail Brown."

The words landed like a weight dropped into the center of the room. Albert froze, every line of his body tensing, as if some invisible thread had been pulled tight.

For a moment, he didn't speak. Then slowly, he straightened in his seat, his voice lower, uncertain.

"And you think I would know the answer to that?" he asked, with a hint of incredulity. But the edge to his tone was more uncertain than defensive—more a question of why than denial.

Jack didn't blink. "You were in the house at the time of the murder."

"That doesn't mean I killed her," Albert said quickly, the words spilling out faster than before, betraying a flicker of panic beneath the surface. His posture shifted, a barely noticeable tightening of the shoulders, the flex of a hand against his thigh. He was holding something in. Or back.

Marion took a small step forward, her eyes fixed on him. "So, you're saying you didn't do it?"

Albert met her gaze, more defiant now. "Of course I didn't do it."

"Why should we believe you?" she asked, her voice cool, almost clinical.

Albert's expression turned pleading for a moment, his composure slipping just slightly. "Because I wouldn't do such a thing."

"But you were in the house," she said. "That puts you closer to the crime than most."

"I didn't hurt her," Albert insisted. "I had no reason to."

207

Marion didn't respond right away. She just looked at him, and in her silence, there was pressure. Expectation.

Finally, she spoke again, calm and precise. "Then what were you doing in the house?"

He hesitated. The pause was long enough to matter. Then, reluctantly, almost as if dragged by invisible strings, he said, "I was in this room. Having an argument."

Jack straightened slightly, his interest piqued. "With who?"

Albert sighed, deeply. "Uriah."

Marion's brow furrowed, her voice dipping lower. "About what?"

Albert waved a hand vaguely in the air, dismissing it.

"Nothing important."

Jack took a step forward, his voice firm now, pushing past civility. "Mr. Oliver…"

Albert's eyes flashed. His voice rose, strained. "It's nothing. Really."

The air grew thicker. Time seemed to stretch between them. Then Marion moved again—

208

closer, slower, and took the seat beside him. Her body language shifted, easing, inviting trust.

"Albert," she said, her voice quieter now, filled with an empathy that felt disarming, "I know you don't think we mean you any harm... Do you?"

Albert looked at her for a long moment. And something in his shoulders released, just a little. "I don't."

"Then just tell us what happened," she said gently. "We won't judge you. And nothing you say will ever leave this room."

There was a moment—perhaps two—where Albert seemed to wrestle with himself, caught between what he knew and what he feared saying. His hands fidgeted slightly in his lap. His gaze flicked to Jack, then to Marion, and back again. They waited, unwavering. They were not angry. They were not pressing him. But they were firm. Steady. Present.

Finally, with a long, tired breath, Albert spoke. His voice was barely above a whisper, as though the very act of saying it aloud burdened him more than anything else.

"Alright, very well," he murmured. "Uriah told Mr. Brown that he was going to check on Abigail after she left the room."

The silence that followed was different than before— charged, electric. Jack and Marion exchanged a glance, wordless but vivid. The walls had not yet given up all their secrets. But a crack had been made.

And through it, the truth was beginning to show.

Albert sat stiffly in the high-backed dining chair, his hands resting uneasily on his lap, fingers twitching every so often as though they wished to form words of their own. The quiet of the room was no longer neutral—it had begun to stretch into something more pronounced, more oppressive. It pressed in from the corners, folding around them like the slow descent of dusk. Marion remained by the doorway, her arms loosely crossed over her waist, but her posture was anything but casual. She watched him with the patience of someone who had waited years for someone else's walls to fall. Jack, meanwhile, stood just beside the edge of the table, his frame stiff but his expression calm, the unwavering attention in his eyes fixed solely on Albert.

210

For a long moment, Albert said nothing. His face betrayed little, save for the way his jaw had clenched and his lips had drawn into a thin line. But when he finally spoke, it was with the tone of someone who had fought against the tide of memory and lost. "I was telling Uriah that what he was doing wasn't right," he said, each word seemingly forced through his teeth as though reluctant to leave the safety of his mind. "I was so angry. More than I'd expected to be."

His voice cracked slightly near the end, and something in his eyes shifted — glazed over, perhaps, not with tears, but with the dull shine of recollection. In that moment, it was clear that Albert was no longer entirely in the present.

Jack's voice came gently, deliberately measured. "What exactly had Uriah done?"

Albert lifted his eyes slowly, and for the first time that evening, something sharp glinted behind his otherwise weary gaze. "He hadn't been honest with her. With Abigail." His voice was thick with contempt — though whether it was for his brother or himself was not immediately clear. "He never cared for her, not truly. Not in the way she thought. Uriah only saw the name she carried. The inheritance. The

211

status." He let out a breath that sounded more like a confession. "We both did, if I'm being truthful. But at least I had the decency to feel ashamed."

Marion stepped forward slightly, her voice softening.

"And she heard the conversation between you two?"

He gave a small, resigned nod. "Yes, every word."

Silence fell again like a guillotine. The weight of what he'd just admitted reverberated through the room. Albert closed his eyes briefly, as though the memory itself were too painful to hold open.

"She was just outside the room. I don't think Uriah saw her, but I did. She must've come down the stairs while we were arguing. She stood by the door, just... still. Frozen. I'll never forget the look on her face. Shock. Betrayal. The sort of pain that hits you in the stomach before it makes it to your heart. And then she was gone. Didn't say a word."

Marion moved slowly to the empty chair beside him and sat down, the proximity a silent offer of support. "You really do try to look after your brother," she said quietly, not accusing, just observant.

Albert gave a half-hearted shrug, but the weariness in his posture said more than his words. "He's my brother. If the Oliver name is going to survive, it has to go through him."

Jack offered a small smile, hopeful, but knowing. "You'll have a family of your own one day. It's not too late."

Albert's face darkened, his jaw stiffened again. "No," he said, almost inaudibly. "I won't."

The simplicity of the statement held finality, and Marion's curiosity sparked at the edge of her expression. She leaned in just a little.

"Why do you say that?" asked Marion.

Albert was hesitant, but he exhaled and spoke, "You can't know what it's like for a man like me…to know that you'll go through this cold world alone."

Jack and Marion exchanged knowing glances. Albert continued.

"Nobody else knows about me. You remember what they did to that Oscar Wilde over in

England all those years ago? I used to wish I could change, you know? Be like everybody else. But I got a right to walk on this earth, just as much as anybody."

Albert sat up sternly in his chair.

"I like who I am and I don't care for anybody that don't approve."

Jack felt his passion, but he did not know how to respond to Albert's decree. He decided to shift back to the matter at hand.

"So, you didn't kill Abigail?"

"No, but she's probably better off."

"Why?" Marion asked in shock.

"She got away from my brother."

Marion's shock softened and she nodded. She placed her hand on his shoulder.

"I believe you."

"Thank you. I think I'll leave now," Albert said.

He hesitated — not because he didn't know the answer, but because he wasn't sure whether it was safe to say it aloud. But then, perhaps remembering Marion's earlier words — nothing you say will leave this room — he finally found the courage to look her in the eye.

"You don't know what it's like to be a man like me," he said, the words quiet, fragile. "To walk through the world each day knowing that even if you live your life gently, carefully, there will still be people ready to tear you down for who you are when the mask slips."

Jack stood a little straighter. Marion didn't speak, not yet.

"I used to pray that I'd change," Albert continued.

"That I could be like everyone else. Marry a nice girl, make my father proud, uphold the family name. But those prayers were lies, and I stopped saying them a long time ago. I am who I am. And I've made peace with that."

He exhaled, long and low, as though the words themselves had exhausted him. "Let the world condemn me if it wants. I won't apologize for being honest anymore."

Marion reached out slowly, placing her hand gently over his arm. "You don't have to," she

215

said, her voice warm and unwavering. "Not here. Not to us."

Albert's expression softened for the first time that night. His lips parted slightly, as though he meant to speak, but instead he simply gave a nod of gratitude. He rose to his feet, reaching for the cane that leaned against the table, and paused for a moment, as though gathering himself before facing the world again.

"I think I'll take my leave," he murmured.

He extended his hand toward Marion first. She rose and took it with quiet dignity. Then, turning to Jack, Albert hesitated for a heartbeat before extending his hand again. Jack accepted it without reservation, their handshake brief but sincere.

As he reached the threshold of the dining room, Albert glanced back, a faint smirk curling at the corners of his mouth.

"You know what the funny thing is?" he said, tilting his head slightly.

Marion looked at him curiously. "What's that?"

"I don't really need this cane."

Jack's eyebrows arched. "Then what do you carry it for?"

Albert lifted the cane, gripping it by the middle and giving it a small, almost theatrical swing through the air.

"Comes in handy when someone needs reminding not to step too far out of line." His eyes sparkled with a flicker of mischief. "And besides, it suits me. Gives me style."

With that, he turned and walked out, the tapping of the cane now rhythmic and deliberate—less necessity, more performance. The man had left more behind in that room than he had taken with him.

Marion moved to Jack's side, her gaze lingering on the now-empty doorway.

"Well," she said, her voice hushed, "that's two down."

Jack reached for her hand, threading his fingers through hers with a quiet sigh. "And two to go."

They stood together for a moment, grounded in the silence, the storm behind them only momentarily passed.

217

Then, from the parlor, raised voices erupted — sharp, angry, unmistakably volatile.

Without a word, Marion and Jack rushed toward the sound, bracing themselves for the next fracture of truth waiting to be exposed.

The moment Jack and Marion crossed the threshold of the parlor, they were immediately engulfed by a maelstrom of disorder and fury. The atmosphere inside had shifted violently from the oppressive quiet of secrets to the explosive aftermath of confrontation. In the center of the room, Winston Brown, his complexion mottled with rage, had both fists curled into the lapels of his son Matthew's jacket. His shoulders trembled with fury as he shook the young man with such force that the seams of the fabric strained and a button clattered to the hardwood floor like a gunshot. His booming voice echoed against the ornate walls, raw with betrayal.

"How dare you say something like that!" Winston's voice erupted, venomous and unrestrained, his face mere inches from Matthew's. "My own son — how dare you!"

Despite the violence of the gesture, Matthew stood his ground, his body rocked but not broken. His features were taut with defiance,

218

chin set, jaw clenched, eyes blazing with a conviction that had clearly been building over time. There was no fear in his expression—only the steel of a long-held truth finally tearing free of its restraints.

Across the room, George stumbled forward, his voice rising in desperation as he reached for Winston's arm.

"Winston! Stop—please, that's enough!" But Winston, deafened by his own outrage, clung tighter to Matthew's coat, unmoved by George's pleas.

On either side of the scuffle, Uriah and Reverend Meadows strained to get a grip on Matthew, each man clutching one of his arms in a frantic attempt to create space between father and son. The room crackled with tension, the chaotic scene unfolding like a storm set loose in the confines of a drawing room.

"It's true!" Matthew's voice cut through the clamor, fierce and trembling, thick with pain that had been long silenced. "You know it is! It's always been true!"

Then came a pause. A breath. A moment of awful anticipation.

Winston's right hand slowly drew back, fingers curling into a tight, trembling fist. The gesture was deliberate, dangerous — charged with intent.

Jack didn't wait. He surged across the room, his voice sharp and urgent. "Winston, no!" he cried, just as the elder Brown's arm began its arc forward. In one swift motion, Jack caught the older man's wrist, gripping it with both hands and forcing the blow downward before it could land. For a second, their eyes locked — Winston's wide with disorientation, as though shocked not only by Jack's intervention, but by the fact that he had truly meant to strike his son.

Then, with a growl more of frustration than surrender, Winston shoved Matthew away. The younger man staggered backward, tripping over the edge of the rug and collapsing to the floor with a heavy thud. He lay there winded, coughing slightly, one arm braced against the carpet as he tried to sit up.

But it was Winston who drew everyone's alarm.

The patriarch reeled back a step, suddenly unsteady, his hand flying to his chest as though something had pierced him from within. His

220

breath grew erratic, short and gasping, his complexion fading from red to a ghastly gray.

"I can't... breathe..." he wheezed, voice thinning to a fragile whisper.

The room collectively froze. Then—

"Winston!" Mabel screamed, her voice raw with fear. She shot to her feet, both hands flying to her mouth. Her face had gone ashen.

"Oh my God— he's taken a turn for the worse!"

She turned abruptly, pointing a trembling hand at Jim, the young college boy who had been standing near the entrance, paralyzed by the eruption of chaos.

"Young man—go! Run and get Dr. Ritter! He's next door—the blue house, go!"

The words had barely left her lips when Jim bolted from his place. He turned and dashed out of the room, his footsteps pounding through the hall, followed by the slam of the front door as he vanished into the night.

Back in the parlor, Reverend Meadows took charge with calm authority.

"Let's get him to the couch," he commanded, stepping forward. George and Jack were already moving, each catching Winston beneath an arm as the older man's knees buckled. Together, they guided him with care and urgency toward the wide velvet couch, where Mabel and Sarah frantically cleared space.

"Loosen his clothing," Meadows instructed as they gently lowered Winston onto the cushions.

George fumbled with the buttons on Winston's jacket, his fingers unsteady. Jack leaned in close, unfastening the collar and top buttons of Winston's shirt, revealing the heaving rise and fall of a chest now straining for every breath. The older man's eyes fluttered, his face glistening with sweat, limbs slack.

Marion had already moved to the nearby serving cart. She soaked a cloth in cool water and returned to kneel beside the couch, dabbing gently at Winston's forehead with a touch that was both practical and compassionate.

The room was heavy with silence now — not the uncomfortable silence of earlier secrets, but the suspended, dread-filled quiet of life hanging in the balance. No one dared speak. Even the usual creaks of the old house seemed to still in reverence to the moment, as though the walls themselves were waiting.

CHAPTER 13

JACK

Outside, under a moonlit sky smothered by clouds, Jim tore across the short yard separating the Brown estate from the blue-painted house next door. His legs pumped furiously beneath him, heart hammering in his chest, lungs burning from both speed and fear. He bounded up the porch steps two at a time and pounded his fists against the front door with desperate urgency.

"Dr. Ritter!" he shouted, voice cracking.

He waited only a second before hammering again, louder and more frantically now, palms smacking against the wood with a steady rhythm of panic. "Please, sir — it's Mr. Brown! You've got to come!"

The door flew open so abruptly that Jim stumbled backward, startled.

Standing there was Dr. Alvin Ritter, a tall African American man in his late forties, with a commanding presence even in his sleep shirt. His deep brown skin glistened with the remnants of sleep, and the faint gleam of silver rimmed his glasses. His eyebrows furrowed, annoyed and confused.

"What is it? What do you want, young man?" he barked, his voice sharp with irritation.

But when Jim stammered, "It's Mr. Brown — sir, he can't breathe — you have to come quick," the doctor's demeanor changed in an instant.

The irritation vanished, replaced by clear-eyed urgency. Dr. Ritter's back straightened. His nostrils flared slightly, already calculating the possibilities.

"I'll get my bag," he said at once, and turned without another word, vanishing into the darkened house.

Jim stood there, still breathless on the porch, staring wide-eyed back across the lawn toward the faint golden glow spilling from the parlor windows. Somewhere inside that house, Winston Brown—the pillar of the family, the unbending spine of tradition—lay struggling for air. And now, like everything else that had been carefully hidden in the shadows of that home, his vulnerability was no longer a secret.

The parlor, only moments ago a cauldron of unrestrained chaos and confrontation, now settled into a tense, breathless quiet. The fury that had gripped every corner of the room had dissolved, replaced by a slow-creeping dread that gnawed at the edges of everyone's composure. Winston Brown, the once-commanding patriarch, now lay stretched across the length of the parlor couch like a broken monument—his face ashen, his shirt clinging damply to his chest, and his breathing reduced to shallow, ragged whispers. A man who once roared like thunder now seemed barely held together by threadbare strength.

Jack was kneeling beside him, his hand gently anchored on Winston's shoulder, steadying him more out of instinct than efficacy.

George stood at the ready just beside them, his face pale but composed, though the tremor in his fingers betrayed the war raging just beneath the surface of his practiced calm.

Around them, the rest of the room held its collective breath, as if fearing that even the smallest noise might tip the balance toward something irreversible.

Mabel's voice, sharp and authoritative though barely concealing the panic coiling inside her, pierced the silence. "Will you men please take him upstairs?" she demanded, not as a plea but as an order—one rooted in the desperation of a woman watching her husband slip through her fingers.

George didn't hesitate. "Will do, Mabel," he answered, his voice tight but determined. "Come on here, Winston." He bent with Jack, both men moving with the delicate precision of those who understood the weight of what they were lifting. Winston groaned faintly—more a whisper of pain than a protest—as his body was raised from the couch.

227

They had barely begun when the front door flew open with a bang, letting in a sharp gust of air that sent a shiver rippling through the room. All heads turned as Jim, breathless and flushed from the run, appeared in the threshold beside a tall, commanding figure—a man whose very presence seemed to hush the air around him.

"I've brought him!" Jim cried, his chest heaving, eyes wide.

The man beside him stepped forward with calm but urgent purpose. He was in his middle years, with deep brown skin, a neatly trimmed mustache, and the unmistakable look of a man accustomed to emergency.

In one hand he carried a thick leather medical bag that looked almost too heavy for its size, and in his eyes— behind a pair of sharp spectacles — burned a sense of immediate responsibility.

"Thank God," Mabel breathed, more to herself than anyone else.

Dr. Alvin Ritter moved swiftly, stepping into the center of the room without hesitation. His eyes scanned the parlor with methodical calculation until they landed on Winston. Without a word, he knelt beside the couch and opened his bag, hands already retrieving the familiar instruments of his trade—his stethoscope, a small tongue depressor, a blood pressure cuff. The family gave him space, parting around him like ripples from a stone.

He worked in silence, his brow furrowed, his fingers moving with the fluidity of muscle memory. He checked Winston's pulse, pressed the stethoscope to his chest, studied the fluttering of his eyelids, and listened carefully to the jagged rhythm of his breathing.

After a moment, he sat back on his heels, his mouth drawn into a tight line.

"It's just as I suspected," he murmured.

"What?" Marion stepped forward, her voice barely above a whisper.

Dr. Ritter turned his gaze toward her. "He's having a heart attack."

The words fell like lead in the center of the room, sinking instantly into the silence. Gasps echoed, as though the truth had struck each person individually.

"Oh my God!" Mabel cried, her hands flying to her chest as if to shield herself from the inevitability of it.

Dr. Ritter was already moving again, standing quickly and issuing orders. "The best thing we can do now is get him to a hospital immediately."

Sarah, her arms folded tight against her chest and her jaw clenched, spoke up from near the fireplace. "The closest one is ten miles away."

"Then we must get him there," Dr. Ritter insisted, his voice unwavering.

But Sarah's reply came quietly, and with a different kind of weight. "They don't take colored patients."

The words were like a cold slap against the warm glow of urgency, and for a moment, even Dr. Ritter faltered. His jaw twitched, and in his eyes, a familiar bitterness briefly rose — but only briefly. The doctor straightened his spine, steadied his voice, and offered no room for despair.

"Then we have no choice," he said firmly. "I'll have to operate."

The declaration landed like thunder rolling through a valley. The very walls of the house seemed to still in its wake.

"Operate? Now?" Mabel blinked, as though she couldn't fully grasp what he was proposing.

"I'm afraid it must be done, Mrs. Brown," Dr. Ritter said, his voice grave but clear. "Your husband is suffering from cardiac ischemia — a dangerous reduction of blood flow to the heart caused by blocked arteries. If we do not intervene within the next hour, I cannot guarantee he'll make it through the night."

Mabel's face crumpled, her lips parting in shock. "Oh no…"

"It was brought on by extreme stress. Did something happen?" Dr. Ritter asked, casting a glance around the room.

There was a collective pause, and all eyes turned to Matthew — who stood stiffly against the far wall, arms at his sides, gaze fixed on the floor.

"Yes," Mabel said, her voice bitter and heavy. "Something happened."

Dr. Ritter didn't ask further. "Then let's not waste any more time. We move him upstairs!"

231

"Very well—George, Jack," Mabel instructed again, this time her voice regaining its earlier strength, drawn from sheer necessity.

The two men once more took hold of Winston, this time with greater urgency, lifting him carefully as Dr. Ritter led the way. Mabel followed close behind, her steps brisk and resolute, lifting the hem of her dress to keep pace. Fear lived behind her eyes, but she did not let it dictate her actions.

Halfway up the stairs, Dr. Ritter paused and looked over his shoulder. "I'm afraid I must do this alone, Mrs. Brown."

"I'm not leaving my husband, Doctor," she replied flatly, steel in her spine. "I want to be in that room."

He considered her, offered a wordless nod. "Then you'll assist."

He looked back over the gathered faces below. "I'll also need help with the instruments."

His eyes found Matthew.

"You—weren't you in medical school?"

Matthew looked up, startled. "Yes. But I dropped out."

"Then you still know enough to be useful. Come along."

Matthew hesitated, visibly wrestling with something inside. He didn't move. The silence that followed was thick with judgment and hope.

Dr. Ritter's eyes narrowed slightly. "Aren't you coming? This may be your only chance to save your father's life, son."

Matthew didn't respond. Mabel walked up to him and slapped him across the face.

"Now you listen, and you listen good," she said. Her eyes were filled with a stern yet quiet rage.

"You and your father may not get along, but I will not allow you to be responsible for his death. He gave you life…now you *will* save his. Is that understood?"

Matthew looked away from her as he massaged his jaw. Mabel asked again in a lower tone.

"I said is that understood?"

With pain and reluctance in his eyes, Matthew paused. However, he eventually walked over to Dr. Ritter. The doctor gave a nod of approval and continued upward. Matthew followed. Mabel cast a brief glance over her shoulder.

"Marion…Sarah…will you—?"

She didn't need to finish. Both women nodded, their eyes wide but resolute, and moved to follow.

As they disappeared up the stairs, the house below fell into a solemn hush, the kind that settles when all action has been taken and only fate remains.

Those left behind stood still, suspended in the uncertain tension of aftermath—haunted by what had been said, and fearful of what still might come.

And upstairs, the night prepared to gamble with life, stitched together by steady hands, a mother's fury, and a son's reluctant return.

CHAPTER 14

MARION

The air in the bedroom was thick—almost suffocating with silence and dread. It wasn't just the quiet that pressed in from all sides, but something heavier, something intangible: the weight of unspoken fears and fragile hopes, the kind of presence that made every breath feel like a prayer.

The single overhead bulb glowed with a muted yellow hue, casting warped shadows along the floral wallpaper and the hardwood floor, lending the space an eerie stillness, like the pause between lightning and thunder.

Winston Brown lay motionless on the bed, his body sunk into the mattress like a man already halfway between this world and the next. His chest, now bare, rose and fell in slow, shallow rhythms, each breath seeming to cost him effort.

Beneath the amber glow, his skin looked almost translucent, drained of the robust color that once signified his authority and fire. His lips had a faint bluish tinge. A folded shirt rested on the nightstand beside him, neatly arranged as if such order could somehow impose calm over the disorder threatening to swallow the night. A damp cloth had been laid across his forehead, already losing its chill.

Across the room, Mabel sat at her vanity, her back rigid, her shoulders held in a posture of defiance against her own rising panic. But her reflection in the mirror betrayed her — there was no fire in those eyes tonight, only grief and helplessness.

The glass captured more than her: behind her, mirrored in silent testament, were the forms of her husband, pale and vulnerable; Dr. Ritter, poised and commanding; and Matthew, a reluctant son standing at the crossroads of fear and redemption. Sarah and Marion stood on

236

either side of Mabel, holding her hands — one each — like sentinels keeping her anchored, their own expressions taut with worry and quiet resolve.

Dr. Alvin Ritter, standing at the foot of the bed with his sleeves rolled up and the glint of resolve in his eyes, spoke in a low, unwavering tone. "I've given Mr. Brown a barbiturate to keep him fully sedated. He won't feel what's coming, and that is crucial. The body can withstand much, but pain can unseat even the strongest will. We cannot risk it."

His words, clinical and calm, still felt like the toll of a distant bell — both reassuring and ominous. With fluid movements, he pulled the surgical mask over his face, the fabric snapping into place, and tugged on his gloves, each rubbery stretch signaling the gravity of what was about to unfold.

Mabel, rising from her seat in a rustle of fabric and purpose, turned to him. Her voice came out barely more than a whisper, but it cut through the hush like a blade. "Do what you must, Dr. Ritter. Please...just bring him back."

Dr. Ritter gave a subtle, respectful nod. "Very well, then. Matthew — scalpel."

Matthew blinked as if roused from a dream. He moved mechanically toward the medical bag at Dr. Ritter's side, fumbling slightly before retrieving the gleaming blade. His fingers shook as he passed it forward, the weight of what it meant suddenly pressing into his very bones.

Dr. Ritter took it without a word, turning to the motionless body of Winston. For a moment, he simply stared at the man's chest, perhaps drawing breath, perhaps praying in the quiet recesses of his own mind.

Then, with a surgeon's precision, he made the first incision — clean, swift, decisive.

The cut parted the flesh, releasing a small, glistening pool of blood that quickly welled up. Dr. Ritter worked fast, clearing it, then cutting through the cartilage with controlled force, fashioning an opening — what he would later refer to as a "trapdoor" — into the chest cavity. The rhythmic thump of Winston's heart became visible: faltering, fragile, yet miraculously still fighting.

"Retractor," Dr. Ritter instructed.

Matthew handed the next tool, still silent, every breath short, as if he feared that even exhaling too loudly might tip the balance between life and death. The retractor was inserted and adjusted. The wound opened further, exposing the pulsating, damaged heart. All the while, the overhead light hummed faintly, the only sound aside from the occasional clink of metal against metal and the deliberate rhythm of surgical motion.

Mabel, Sarah, and Marion remained where they were, their expressions frozen in a kind of collective stasis. Sarah whispered soft verses beneath her breath, and Marion rubbed slow, firm circles against Mabel's back, her eyes wet but unblinking.

"Forceps," Dr. Ritter murmured, his voice steady, locked in the rhythm of the procedure.

Another instrument changed hands. Then another.

And another.

Time unraveled. What might have been minutes stretched into eternities. No one dared to move, let alone speak.

Dr. Ritter's hands moved with astonishing control, as if guided by something beyond training — by a sheer, unshakable will to preserve

239

life. He worked along the arteries, isolating the blockage, clearing the clots, reinforcing the vessel walls with the skill of a man who had done this in far worse conditions.

When the worst was over, Dr. Ritter leaned back slightly, his breathing heavier now, the tension in his shoulders betraying the toll it had taken. His gloved fingers were slick with sweat and blood. And still, Winston's chest rose and fell, steady now—still faint, but no longer faltering.

"I'll rinse now," he said quietly.

Matthew, now visibly shaken, handed over a small vial of sterilizing solution, and Dr. Ritter dabbed the wound clean with practiced care. The color of Winston's skin had begun to change, ever so subtly—less ashen, more flushed.

"Needle and thread," Dr. Ritter said.

Matthew handed over the suture kit, his fingers brushing the doctor's gloved hands with a faint tremor. Dr. Ritter didn't look up. He threaded the needle and began stitching, slow and deliberate, each loop a fragile hope tethering Winston to life.

Snip. The final thread was trimmed.

Dr. Ritter let out a breath — deep and weary.

Mabel stepped forward, her hands clutching each other so tightly her knuckles had turned white. "Is it... is it done?"

Dr. Ritter peeled his mask down. His eyes met hers — tired, yes, but clear and sure.

"The surgery is complete," he said. "He survived it.

Your husband did well."

The words dropped into the room like a stone into still water. Mabel's legs buckled slightly as Sarah and

Marion caught her. Mabel burst into soft sobs. The long-held breath of the room seemed to finally release itself.

"Hallelujah," Sarah whispered, eyes turned upward.

"Amen," Marion murmured, voice cracking with relief.

Dr. Ritter removed his gloves with slow precision, tossing them into the metal basin with a soft clink. He wiped his brow with the back of his sleeve and glanced around the room.

241

"I must be frank — this isn't a victory, not yet. He is alive, yes, but what comes next will be just as critical. He'll need rest. No stress. No sudden movements. He must be guarded like a porcelain vase. His heart has endured too much already."

Mabel stepped to the bedside and took Winston's limp hand into hers. She lowered her head and pressed her forehead gently against his knuckles, her breath warm and steady.

"If it's all right," she said after a moment, her voice hushed and raw, "I would prefer to stay with him tonight."

Dr. Ritter nodded solemnly. "Yes, Mrs. Brown. That would be most appropriate."

Marion got up and walked over to Sarah. Sarah grinned like a happy schoolgirl as the two hugged and watched Winston being tended to by Mabel.

Marion and Sarah decided to leave the room, allowing Winston to rest. While out of the room, Marion stopped Sarah in the hall saying, "That was a stressful experience."

Sarah shook her head in agreement.

"Oh Lord, I thought I was the only one thinking that. Even with all I've been through as a midwife, I was sweating Marion. I swear!"

Marion nodded.

"Yes, tonight has been a true test of my spirit. I prayed more tonight than I ever did."

Sarah laughed. "I didn't know you had so little faith?"

"Oh no, it was just an expression."

"Still, this night has been a nightmare."

"You're right," Marion said, placing her hands on her hips.

"What's happening to this city? All this evil and misfortune! If only that fight hadn't happened…"

Marion looked back at the closed door leading to Winston's room. She got closer to Sarah and asked suddenly, "What really started that fight anyways?"

Sarah opened her mouth, but quickly closed it as she looked away somewhat embarrassed.

"Well, all of us were there and we just started talking about Abigail. We were discussing all the things we remembered about her. It was just some of us recounting some of those fond moments. That's all."

Marion asked, "And how did those two get into it?" Sarah sighed. "Matthew…was talking. It was after Winston spoke about her. Matthew just jumped in and talked about her quite negatively. It just wasn't right. It really wasn't, Marion."

"Let me guess, Winston got mad?"

Sarah nodded. "Winston told Matthew to silence himself.

Matthew continued then he said it." "What?"

"That Abigail was always his favorite. That he was treated like a hog compared to…Abigail the princess."

Marion was shocked. No wonder Winston lost it. Though, if that were true, that meant there had been resentment between the two for a long time.

Matthew dropping out of school just made it worse.

Sarah continued, "All hell broke loose after that. It was chaos. The two were just hauling insults at each other. I really hope they stay strong and stay away from hating one another.

They need each other more than ever now that Abigail is gone."

Marion sighed and nodded in agreement. "Yes, Matthew is their only child now."

The bedroom door suddenly opened. Dr. Ritter exited the room with Matthew following. Marion turned towards him. Before long, they all descended the staircase and were soon at the bottom of the stairs in the foyer.

CHAPTER 15

JACK

One by one, the members of the household descended the staircase, their steps slow and heavy, each movement burdened by the weight of fatigue and the emotional toll of the night. The upstairs bedroom, bathed in dim amber light, was left behind with its door slightly ajar, a quiet sentinel over the room where Winston Brown now lay in the first restful sleep he had known in what felt like an eternity. His breathing, though faint and shallow, held a steadiness that had been absent for hours. Mabel sat beside him, her form hunched gently over the edge of the bed, her fingers loosely curled around her husband's hand. She watched him not with fear, but with quiet reverence, as though bearing witness to a miracle still unfolding.

Downstairs, in the parlor where time seemed to have stilled, everyone gradually gathered, their faces glowing and drawn beneath the soft light of the gas lamps. The long vigil had left its mark—shoulders slumped with exhaustion, eyes red-rimmed from both tears and sleeplessness. Jack and George entered last, their boots scuffing softly against the wooden floor as they joined the solemn cluster already assembled near the hearth. No one spoke immediately. It was the kind of silence that didn't demand to be filled, only understood—shared in its heaviness.

Marion was the first to break it, turning toward Dr. Alvin Ritter, who now stood near the front door, methodically pulling on his overcoat with a calm that had been his armor through the night's ordeal. He adjusted the leather strap of his medical bag, the weight of it shifting slightly in his hand. Marion's voice, though weary, carried a warmth and sincerity that momentarily pierced the stillness. "Thank you very much, Dr. Ritter, for coming on such short notice," she said, her gaze steady, the edges of her mouth twitching toward a grateful smile that didn't quite reach her eyes.

Dr. Ritter, ever modest, gave a casual wave of his gloved hand, brushing off the praise with a humility that seemed genuine. "Oh, don't thank me," he said, his voice low and even, like a man used to speaking in hushed rooms where life and death mingled. "If you're going to thank anyone, thank Dr. Daniel Hale Williams. He's the one who made this even remotely possible—a remarkable man, back in the 1890s. Negro surgeon. Performed one of the first successful heart surgeries on record. Paved the way for the rest of us. I'm just treading the ground he broke open."

He turned his eyes to Marion, and then to Sarah, offering each of them a brief, solemn nod. "To tell you the truth," he added, "it's not just him. It's the two of you who helped tonight. Keeping Mrs. Brown steady— keeping the room steady—that matters more than you might think."

Sarah, who had been standing beside the piano with her arms folded against her chest, gave a modest shrug, downplaying the weight of her own presence. "It was no big thing," she murmured, though her voice betrayed a thread of emotion that hadn't quite unraveled.

Dr. Ritter allowed himself a faint smile — a rare softness creasing the lines of his face. "Well, nonetheless," he replied gently, "it mattered."

His eyes swept the room once more, settling finally on Matthew, who had remained quiet, a few steps back from the rest, near the foot of the staircase. The young man's posture was rigid, his hands tucked deep into his pockets, but there was something in his expression — something raw and quiet — that caught the doctor's attention.

"I heard from the boy who came to fetch me," Dr. Ritter said carefully, his voice gentler now, "about what happened to Abigail?"

Matthew's head lowered slightly at the mention of her name, as though a wave of memory had struck him hard in the chest. He gave a faint nod, his jaw tight with emotion he refused to show. "Yes, sir," he said simply. "Thank you."

Dr. Ritter gave another nod, one filled with gravity, as if offering a prayer through posture. He turned back to the coat rack, fastening the final clasp of his coat with fingers that now moved a little slower, wearied from the strain of the procedure. For a moment, the room was filled only with the quiet rustle of wool and the soft creak of old wood.

"Well then," he said, slinging his bag over his shoulder, "you all take care now. And mind what I said — absolute rest. That heart's been through more than most can bear."

Sarah offered a faint smile, her voice tender. "You have a good night, Doctor."

With a final nod, Dr. Ritter reached for the brass doorknob, pulled the front door open, and stepped out into the crisp stillness of the predawn dark. The door clicked shut behind him, quiet and final. A few seconds later, his footsteps faded down the walk, swallowed by the silence outside.

And just like that, the long, harrowing night gave way to the hush of its closing moments — a silence not heavy with dread this time, but one that carried the tentative beginnings of peace.

The parlor had fallen into a still, reverent silence. Only the gentle crackling of the fire in the hearth broke through the quiet, a soft, rhythmic pulse that filled the room like the echo of a heartbeat long held in suspense. Shadows from the flames danced across the walls, casting flickering patterns that shifted with every log's subtle pop and sigh. The air, though warm, held a strange hollowness — thick with waiting, with worry, with the residue of fear not yet exhaled.

Sarah, Marion, and Matthew stepped inside the parlor, their faces etched with fatigue, their clothing dusted in the faint, invisible residue of stress and urgency. Their eyes were sunken, their movements slow, but behind the exhaustion, glimmers of hope burned — quiet, but unmistakable.

At once, those who had remained behind stirred from their seats. George rose from his chair near the window; Jack stood from the sofa, hands sliding into his pockets; Uriah, arms crossed, straightened to his full height; Albert looked up from where he had been nursing a lukewarm cup of tea; Mary and Jim stood side by side; and Reverend Meadows, ever poised and composed, took one small step forward. The room breathed in as one, waiting for the words none of them had dared to say aloud.

The silence held until Reverend Meadows finally spoke, his voice steady and low, a thread of reverence woven through it. "Well?" he asked,

251

his eyes resting on Matthew with a gentleness that belied the gravity of the question.

Matthew, standing just past the threshold, took a slow breath. He looked up briefly, then lowered his gaze, his voice barely more than a whisper, raw and almost hollow. "He's fine," he said. "Dr. Ritter performed the surgery. He's going to be alright."

The impact of those words spread through the room like a gust of wind cutting through stagnant air—relief, swift and overwhelming. Jack clapped his hands together with a grin, the sound startling in its cheer. "Well, thank goodness," he exclaimed, exhaling a breath that seemed to release hours of tension.

Albert gave a curt nod, his tone more measured but no less sincere. "Matthew, you must be so relieved."

"Yes...relieved." The word came from Matthew slowly, as though spoken through a throat full of stones. He crossed the room without another glance, his steps dragging slightly, and dropped heavily onto the couch. Elbows braced against his knees, he buried his face in his hands. The room saw only the back of his bowed head, but the posture said enough. The weight pressing on him wasn't just from the long night or from fear—it was something deeper, something quiet and gnawing that pulled at the edges of his soul.

George moved beside Sarah and leaned in close, lowering his voice so that only she could hear. "I think we've had enough excitement for one night, don't you think?"

Sarah gave a faint nod, brushing a strand of hair from her cheek. "Yes," she said. "Let's go home."

George managed a tired smile. "After everything that's happened, you don't have to tell me twice."

He turned to face the others, giving a casual wave of farewell. "Goodnight, everybody."

Sarah lingered. Her hand found Marion's, and she held it tight for a moment. "Take care of them," she said softly, her voice trembling at the edges. "This family's been through so much. A lot of pain under this roof, but... the Browns really are good people. Take care of them."

Marion nodded, her eyes shining with unshed tears, her smile gentle but unwavering. "I will," she promised.

With that, the door closed behind Sarah and George, the click of the latch echoing softly into the hush that followed. One by one, the others began to drift away, the storm of the night now giving way to the gentle pull of home and rest.

Jim placed a hand on Mary's arm. "We better get going too, cousin. Come on."

Mary nodded silently, and the two slipped out without another word.

Albert lingered by the doorway. He glanced back, his expression unreadable, and then looked toward Marion and Jack. "I think it's time for me to go as well," he said. "Mr. and Mrs. Franklin, it was a pleasure meeting you."

He turned to Matthew, whose face was still hidden in his hands. "Matthew," Albert said gently, "I'm sorry for your loss. I'm glad your father is on the mend."

Matthew gave a barely perceptible nod. He did not raise his head.

Albert's eyes slid briefly toward Uriah, studying him, and for the briefest second, something flickered across his face—a thought unspoken. But he said nothing. Marion stepped forward and gave his hand a brief, warm squeeze.

"Take care of yourself," she said.

"I will," Albert replied, then disappeared into the shadows of the porch and into the night beyond.

Reverend Meadows stepped forward, his presence somehow filling the room despite his soft-spoken nature. He stopped near Matthew and Uriah, his eyes resting on them with quiet understanding.

"I'll take my leave, too," he said gently. "Matthew, Uriah...take care. I'll be praying for you both."

He turned to Jack and Marion, shaking each of their hands with practiced grace. Then, drawing them closer with a subtle glance around the room, he lowered his voice to a whisper.

"Mr. and Mrs. Franklin," he said, "good luck."

Jack tilted his head. "Why's that?"

"There's something about that young man Uriah," the reverend said, his voice slow and deliberate. "He seemed...very odd. Especially as Mr. Brown was being operated on."

255

Marion leaned in slightly. "Odd? In what way?"

Reverend Meadows narrowed his eyes, searching for the right words. "He was agitated. Restless. As if he had something to lose if Mr. Brown didn't survive. It struck me as...unsettling."

Jack took in the words, his expression guarded.

"Thank you, Reverend. We'll keep our eyes open."

"We'll do our best to right the wrong that was done here tonight," Marion added quietly.

The reverend gave one final nod, solemn and full of weight. "May God be with you."

And then he, too, slipped away, leaving the parlor in the deepening quiet of its final hour.

Only four remained now: Jack, Marion, Matthew, and Uriah. The fire in the hearth had burned lower, casting long, lazy shadows that flickered across the room like memories too stubborn to fade.

Marion broke the silence, her voice thoughtful, almost distant. "Jack," she said, turning toward him, "I've been thinking about something."

He looked up from his place near the fireplace, where he had been absently watching the flames. "Yes?"

"I've been wondering what Abigail was doing in the library," she said, slowly pacing to the edge of the room.

Jack furrowed his brow. "I don't know. You think she was hiding something?"

"Maybe," Marion murmured, "or maybe she was looking for something that was already hidden."

Jack followed her gaze across the room to where Uriah and Matthew stood in hushed conversation. His expression shifted slightly — calculated now, purposeful.

"Maybe it's time we change our strategy a bit."

Marion turned toward him, intrigued. "What do you suggest?"

"Let's try separating this time," Jack said, rising to his feet. "Divide and conquer."

257

A smile tugged at Marion's lips, despite the tension that still lingered in the room. "Oh? Divide and conquer, is it?"

Jack nodded. "You take Uriah. Talk to him. I'll head into the library. That's where Abigail died — maybe something in there still hasn't come to light."

"I love it when you take charge," Marion said, a glint of affection in her eyes.

Jack offered a quick, rakish grin. She leaned in, kissed him softly on the cheek, and turned toward Uriah, who had just finished speaking with Matthew.

He noticed her approach and straightened. "Are you alright, Mrs. Franklin?" he asked, the concern in his voice polite, but guarded.

"I'm fine," she replied evenly. "But I was hoping I could have a word with you. In private."

Matthew looked between them, then nodded. "Of course. You can use the parlor," he said, beginning to ascend the stairs. "I'll go check on my father."

He offered Marion a respectful look before disappearing up the steps, his footsteps echoing faintly overhead.

Marion turned to Uriah. "Shall we?"

As she led him toward the far side of the room, Jack moved with quiet determination into the hallway, the glow of the hearth behind him dimming with each step. The library door stood ahead like a silent witness, untouched since the tragedy that had changed everything.

And if there were still secrets buried in that room— Jack intended to find them.

The library door groaned softly as Jack eased it open, the hinges protesting against years of neglect and a night steeped in tragedy. The room beyond lay cloaked in shadow, save for a single lamp casting a pool of amber light across the wooden floor. Books lined the walls like silent sentinels, their spines dulled with age, their secrets kept in brittle silence. The air was dense, heavy with the bitter residue of fear and grief. It pressed in on Jack's chest as he stepped inside.

And then—there she was.

Abigail's body, still covered with a white sheet, lay motionless near the hearth. Though he kept his gaze forward, determined not to let it wander, her presence was unavoidable. Death had a way of saturating a place, of rooting itself in the grain of the furniture, in the hush between heartbeats. Jack's steps rang out with quiet resolve as he crossed the room, the silence closing in behind him.

He approached the desk, its surface cluttered with loose pages, a stopped watch, an uncapped fountain pen bleeding dry. His fingers moved with care as he reached for the reading lamp and flicked it on. The bulb buzzed faintly, casting golden light over the chaos. Amid the clutter, an open book rested awkwardly—its spine cracked, its pages splayed wide. Something protruded from its center: a folded slip of paper, yellowed at the corners, delicate from handling.

Jack's heart beat a little faster as he plucked it free.

He unfolded the note with practiced care, smoothing it against the surface of the desk. His eyes scanned the contents—just a few lines, hastily scribbled. But the weight they carried hit him like a blow to the chest. The lines were brief, blunt...and damning.

Whatever this was, it had changed everything.

Across the house, in the stillness of the parlor, a very different battle unfolded.

Marion sat with perfect posture, hands clasped loosely before her, the candlelight glinting off her eyes as she fixed them on the man across from her. Uriah slouched in his chair, a permanent scowl on his face, arms crossed like a child being scolded.

"So you mean to tell me," Marion began, her voice cool and level, "that you had nothing to do with what happened to Abigail?"

Uriah leaned forward, his jaw tight with irritation.

"No. And I don't appreciate you thinkin' I did."

Marion's brow arched. "Then everything your brother, Albert, told us was a lie?"

"Exactly," Uriah shot back.

"Including the part where you lured him here under false pretenses?"

There was a pause. The edge in her tone sharpened the silence between them.

Uriah's eyes darted, his expression faltering just enough for her to notice. The mask slipped.

"Yes," he said, slower now. "Including that."

Marion tilted her head, observing him with new interest. "Funny. He was very convincing when he said it. I believed him."

Uriah scoffed, his lip curling. "You would, wouldn't you?"

Her gaze hardened. "What's that supposed to mean?"

"You women," he muttered darkly, "always so gullible. You'll believe whatever some smooth-talker tells you."

Marion's patience began to fray. "Now listen here-"

"I didn't kill my fiancée," Uriah barked, rising in his seat. "Why don't you stop wasting my time and do something useful—like cleanin' up the kitchen? I'm sure it's a mess after dinner."

Marion stood slowly, fury burning beneath her carefully composed exterior. "I am not your maid. I am a tenured professor at one of the most prestigious universities in the city."

Uriah shrugged with theatrical indifference. "What's wrong with being a maid?"

"Nothing," she shot back, "unless you're the kind of man who thinks that's the only thing women are good for."

He smirked, giving her a slow once-over. "A professor, huh? They must've been real desperate."

Before Marion could find the words she wanted — sharp, elegant, devastating — Jack burst into the room.

"Marion," he said, voice low and urgent. "You have to see this."

She didn't hesitate. She threw Uriah a final look, one brimming with disgust, and followed Jack to a quiet corner near the front door.

He handed her the note. Her eyes scanned it quickly — and widened.

"Oh my God," she breathed.

Jack's mouth was a firm line. "You know what this means, don't you?"

Marion looked up at him, the fire returning to her eyes. "I certainly do."

The grandfather clock in the hallway ticked with slow, solemn rhythm, its chimes long since silenced, leaving only the steady cadence of passing seconds to fill the house. In the dining room, the hush was profound— so complete it felt like something sacred. A single lamp above the table cast a warm but narrow glow, spilling shadows across the walls that twisted and elongated with each flicker of the bulb. The light was dim, reverent, like that of a chapel at dusk.

Marion sat at the head of the table, her hands lightly resting on a single folded letter. The paper, though no longer open, might as well have been carved into the wood—its message etched into her mind with such clarity it seemed she could still hear the words being spoken. Her gaze remained fixed on the surface before her, tracing the grain of the polished mahogany, as though it could anchor her in the storm now gathering beyond the walls.

From the hallway, the faint sound of footsteps broke the stillness.

Jack entered with a quietness that seemed intentional, respectful. His face was pale, drawn tight with fatigue, and yet something more—

restraint, perhaps. The need to keep his thoughts in check.

Marion didn't look up right away. When she finally spoke, her voice was quiet but steady. "Well?"

Jack exhaled as he took the seat beside her, rubbing a hand across his brow as though trying to press away the weight of the evening. "He's on his way," he said simply.

The front foyer remained cloaked in shadow, save for the narrow band of light that stretched from under the dining room door. The air felt heavier there, cooler somehow, like the house itself had begun to hold its breath.

A pair of polished black shoes tapped against the hardwood floor, each step deliberate, echoing faintly with a precision that bordered on ceremonial. The figure moved slowly, not out of hesitation but calculation — every footfall measured, as though each step carried consequence.

He advanced down the corridor toward the dining room, his posture upright, his silhouette unwavering.

The house watched in silence.

CHAPTER 16

MARION

The dining room had taken on a peculiar stillness, not the kind that simply arrives with silence, but one that feels conjured — manufactured by the weight of unspoken truths. The air itself seemed to press inward, heavy with the friction of everything unsaid. Shadows clung to the corners of the room, lengthened by the low amber light cast from a chandelier that swayed ever so faintly, though no breeze stirred. A faint ticking came from the grandfather clock in the hallway, the kind of ticking that felt deliberate —

like the slow counting down of something inevitable.

Marion stood by the far wall, her posture composed but taut, her eyes fixed on the doorway as though she expected it to open at any second. Jack remained seated at the table, hands clasped tightly before him, his brow furrowed in quiet concentration. Between them hung an unspoken understanding: this moment was a threshold. Once crossed, nothing could return untouched.

Then—footsteps. Confident. Measured. Too evenly spaced to belong to someone unsure.

Matthew appeared in the doorway, exactly as he had been throughout the evening, though now the details betrayed him. The charcoal vest, once impeccable, now showed faint creases; his white shirt, though still crisp, bore the telltale signs of long wear—slight wrinkling near the cuffs, the collar slightly loosened as though he'd begun to unravel in private. Under his eyes, the thinnest suggestion of shadow, almost imperceptible, but undeniable. The face was still his, charming and composed, but it felt like a mask that had been worn too long. It no longer sat naturally.

267

He offered a pleasant, practiced smile as he stepped fully into the room. "You wanted to see me?"

Jack gestured silently toward the empty chair across from him. "Have a seat, Matthew."

Marion's voice followed, cool and sharp as the edge of a silver knife. "Please. Join us."

Matthew accepted the invitation with the ease of a man who had long ago learned to make any room his stage. He pulled out the chair with a quiet scrape and lowered himself into it with a grace that bordered on theatrical. Folding his hands neatly on the table before him, he exhaled softly.

"I'm glad the two of you are still here," he said, his tone warm, even appreciative. "It's a comfort, really — to know the family still has such steadfast allies in a time like this."

Marion studied him without blinking. "Is that so?"

"Oh, absolutely," Matthew replied, his smile unwavering. "With everything that's happened... I honestly don't know how we'd manage without you."

There was a calculated gentleness to his tone, but it rang hollow in the quiet of the room. Marion tilted her head slightly, not smiling.

Jack leaned forward then, his voice sharp but calm.

"How's your father?"

Matthew's expression didn't falter, though something in his eyes flickered. "Much better, thank you. Dr. Ritter's been incredible. We're very grateful."

"I imagine your family means a great deal to you," Marion said, her words carefully measured.

Matthew nodded, the gesture slow and deliberate.

"More than anything."

The silence that followed was dense, as though the air itself was bracing for what came next.

Jack's eyes narrowed. His voice was a whisper sharpened into a blade. "Then why did you kill your own sister?"

The question landed with the full weight of a thunderclap, reverberating through the room in a stunned and suffocating silence. It wasn't shouted. It didn't need to be. Its precision was more devastating than volume could ever be.

Matthew blinked slowly, and for a long moment, he didn't speak. His smile dissolved, piece by piece, until what remained was something bare and unsettled. He rose to his feet with slow deliberation, as if pulled upward by disbelief.

"I'm sorry," he said, his voice quiet but brittle. "What did you just say?"

"You heard me," Jack said, unmoving.

Matthew's jaw worked soundlessly for a beat before his features twisted with offense. "I know what you said. And if you had any sense at all, you'd take it back."

Jack didn't so much as blink. His fists were clenched on the table, the bones in his knuckles stark beneath his skin. He looked as though he'd been carved from something solid and immovable. Marion's hand reached out and rested gently on his forearm—a silent check, not of warning, but unity. Then she turned to Matthew, slowly, deliberately, and drew something from her coat pocket.

A folded piece of paper.

Matthew's eyes tracked it like a predator watching a weapon being drawn.

"This," Marion said, her voice unhurried but infused with a chill that cut deeper than accusation, "is what makes us say it."

Matthew's eyes narrowed. "What is that?"

"Don't insult us with questions you already know the answer to."

He reached for the paper, but she stepped back, unfolding it with care and lifting it into the dim light as though unveiling something sacred. Then she began to read, each word deliberate and clipped with the solemnity of an epitaph.

"To Whom It May Concern, I leave this letter in the hopes that it will serve as documentation of my intentions. I have just been given a dire diagnosis that may alter the course of my life. In the process of drafting a will, I leave this letter in the interim and will have it witnessed in the morning..."

Matthew stiffened, a faint tremor running through his spine. His breath stilled in his throat.

271

"What does this have to do with anything?" he asked eventually, though the steel in his voice had dulled.

Jack's reply came soft but firm. "Keep listening."

Marion's eyes did not leave Matthew's face as she read the final lines.

"In the case of my passing, I leave the distribution of my finances and the running of my businesses to my wife Mabel, my daughter Abigail, and her fiancé Uriah. Sincerely, Winston Frederick Brown. May 16th, 1911."

She lowered the page slowly, her fingers still trembling slightly from the tension they carried.

Silence again. Only the faint groan of the house settling and the eternal tick of the hallway clock. Then—"He really didn't leave me anything?" Matthew asked, the question half-spoken to himself. His face had lost its color. The lines at the corners of his mouth now pulled downward in disbelief and something darker.

Jack said to Matthew, "The letter was witnessed by a man named Mr. Benjamin Carter."

Matthew straightened up and planted his arms on his hips. He shook his head in disappointment before answering, "He's my father's lawyer."

"Then this document shows testamentary intent," Marion said, quietly but with authority. "Your father meant for this to be treated as valid until the formal will could be drafted. Legally, it holds weight."

Matthew's eyes flickered again, this time faster. His breath hitched and his jaw clenched.

"So what you're saying," he said, his voice lowering into something colder, "is that he meant to cut me out. Entirely."

Jack said nothing.

Marion leaned forward. Her voice dropped, became a thread pulled taut. "Why is Abigail dead, Matthew?"

His gaze lifted to meet hers — and for the first time, the polish cracked.

"Tell us the truth," she added, her voice now barely above a whisper.

He opened his mouth once, closed it, then opened it again. His throat worked against words he had not yet decided whether to release. A muscle ticked in his cheek. And then, in a voice so low it might have been mistaken for wind:

"I didn't kill my sister...but I know who did."

Every nerve in the room tightened.

Jack leaned in. Marion followed. Their voices, united, came soft and sharp:

"Who?"

The parlor sat in an oppressive stillness, cloaked in shadows that stretched across the faded wallpaper like ghostly fingers. The only sound breaking the silence was the slow, stubborn ticking of the mantel clock — each second peeling away with torturous patience, like the beat of a condemned man's heart. Uriah sat rigid in his high-backed chair, his hands clenched tightly around the armrests. A sense of unease had slithered into the room and coiled itself around him. His mind, once lulled into a dazed quiet, now flickered with questions that refused to be silenced. Where had everyone gone? Why was the house so suddenly cold?

With a sharp breath, he stood. The silence felt too full, too deliberate — as if the walls themselves were listening. The moment demanded motion,

274

demanded answers. He stepped out of the parlor and into the hallway, where the shadows only deepened.

The corridor was dim and cool, lined with portraits of long-dead ancestors whose eyes seemed to follow Uriah as he moved. The chill in the air crept into his bones, making his skin bristle. He paused mid-step, ears straining as a sound pierced the quiet—a low murmur, voices carried from behind the dining room door. The words were muffled, but the tension in them was unmistakable.

He moved closer, each footstep softened by the thick Persian rug beneath him. He pressed his back against the wall beside the dining room entrance, breath held tight. His heart quickened, pounding now with a kind of dread he hadn't yet named.

Uriah's breath caught.

"It was Uriah," came Matthew's voice—flat, cold, and cutting.

The name fell like a guillotine blade. A rush of panic surged through Uriah, visceral and immediate. He didn't pause to think. Instinct took over, and his hand shot out, grasped the

275

doorknob, and shoved the heavy door open with a force that startled even him.

Warm, amber light bled across the dining room, catching the polished wood of the table and the crystal decanter resting like a sentinel beside half-full glasses. Marion and Jack stood at the far end, their expressions frozen in shock. Matthew sat back in his chair, his face stony, eyes like knives.

"Is everything alright in here?" Uriah asked, the tremor in his voice barely masked by an attempt at casual concern. "I was wondering where everyone had gone."

Jack turned toward him, his expression unreadable. "Matthew was just telling us that he knows who killed his sister."

Uriah felt his chest cave inward. "Does he?"

Marion didn't blink. "Yes. He does. Go on, Matthew."

Silence fell like snow, muffling breath and thought. All eyes pivoted toward Matthew, whose movements were slow and deliberate as he rose from his chair, never breaking his gaze from Uriah. The weight of his stare pressed down like a stone.

"It was Uriah," he said, voice sharp with certainty.

"That's a lie!" Uriah's voice exploded, shattering the calm. It erupted from him with such force, it startled even Jack. His hands trembled as he stepped back, but he held his ground.

"It is not, and you know it! Tell them!" Matthew's voice was raised now, trembling not with fear, but with fury.

Marion held up a hand, trying to steady the air. "Matthew," she said, her tone level, almost maternal. "How do you know that?"

"I just know, okay?" Matthew barked, his carefully built façade cracking. Anger flickered in his eyes, and something else — desperation, perhaps.

A heavy silence cloaked the room once more, but this time it was heavier, almost unbearable.

And then Uriah spoke.

His voice broke, shattered by the weight of the words before they even left his lips. "Alright," he whispered, and the word felt like a confession wrung from his soul. "It was me. I did it."

Jack staggered back a step, confusion clouding his features. "That doesn't make any sense. Why would you do something like that?"

Uriah turned to Matthew, his jaw tight, eyes red.

"Why don't you ask him?"

All heads turned.

"Matthew?" Jack asked slowly, suspicion building like a rising tide.

Matthew gave a short, mirthless laugh. "Don't listen to him. He's lost it. He's nuts."

Uriah finally looked up at Matthew square in the eyes.

"Just tell them," pleaded Uriah.

"He's nuts! Don't you see? He's nuts," Matthew shouted.

Marion watched them both. She was both confounded and dismayed at the situation. All she knew now was that both were involved in Abigail's death.

"The jig is up, man. They got us," Uriah said with sad finality.

Marion turned to Matthew. "Well...?"

Matthew was hesitant, but he finally admitted to his part in the crime saying, "I had her killed."

Jack shook his head in disappointment. Marion stared into Matthew's eyes, wondering what led to such a horrible action. She was morbidly distraught just looking at them.

"I wanted my sister dead," Matthew continued. "But I couldn't do it myself, so I had Uriah kill her instead."

Marion had to know. "But why?"

"My father's heart was getting weaker and weaker. It was only a matter of time before he was gonna croak. I didn't know if he had made a will or not, but I knew he was gonna leave me out of it."

"Why would you assume that?" asked Jack.

"Because he said it..." Matthew responded with a short tone. "Why would I leave anything to you when you'd just waste everything away. I actually thought he was joking..."

Marion was still perplexed. She asked, "But why Abigail?"

"You've read the letter. My father was going to leave everything to my mom and Abigail. If she wasn't around, then he'd be forced to leave her half to me."

"And me," said Uriah, raising his finger in the air.

Jack scoffed at Uriah's comment.

"What do you mean? You were so broken up when everyone found out she died."

Matthew turned towards Uriah.

"You should've made a career on the stage, old friend," Matthew said with a smirk. Uriah scoffed.

"Don't you "old friend" me. Where's my money?"

Marion leaned forward.

"What are you talking about?"

Uriah gestured towards Marion.

"He promised me he would give me my money if I killed her." Uriah turned once more towards Matthew. "Now, where's my money?"

Matthew stared at Uriah, staying firm in his stance.

"How much did he promise you?" asked Jack.

"Three thousand dollars!" Matthew screamed.

"That's right and I want it all now!" added Uriah.

Matthew was surprisingly calm. Marion was about to interject. However, Matthew continued.

"I never had it."

"What? What do you mean you never had it? I need that money! My family needs that money!" Uriah was hysterical. He couldn't believe what he was hearing.

"Like I said," Matthew coldly stated, "I never had it."

Matthew ignored him and sat down in one of the dining room chairs, unbothered. Marion could see this was going to go south.

Uriah lunged at Matthew in anguish. Jack stopped him, holding him back. They toppled over one another as Matthew sat there not even looking at them. Uriah soon knelt on the floor. He covered his face in his hands and began to weep.

Jack wrapped his arms firmly around Uriah, trying to comfort him.

"Oh, God! What have I done? What have I done?"

Matthew stood up from the dining room chair. He took out a cigarette from the inside pocket of his jacket and lit it. He walked in front of Uriah.

"I'll tell you what you've done," said Matthew. His tone was menacing and cruel. "Thanks to you, I'm free. Free of my sister. She could never do anything wrong in my parents' eyes. I was always the black sheep, you know, but now I'm free of her. The greatest pain a person can feel is loss."

Marion felt an intense searing heat rise from within her. She never thought the day would come when she could hate someone, but it was clear at that moment. She hated Matthew.

How could he have done this? He was an utter monster. Worse than any villain she ever encountered.

Smiling, Matthew turned to Marion.

"What greater pain is there for a parent to feel…than the loss of their own child?"

Jack and Marion were silent, mortified by what had transpired.

"I think it's time for the both of you to go now," Matthew said. He looked down at Uriah. "Oh, and don't forget to take out the trash when you leave."

Matthew walked toward the dining room entrance.

Marion shot up from her seat and bellowed, "You won't get away with this!"

He turned around. "Get away with what? I didn't do anything." He pointed his cigarette down at Uriah. "He did."

Jack stood up in anger. He was furious. He swung and punched Matthew. They struggled, pushing over a chair before Jack was able to push aside Matthew's arm, breaking a vase as he dropped back.

Matthew immediately got up and lunged forward. He landed a hit against the topside of Jack's head.

Marion shivered in fear. Her heart pounded with each terrifying punch that was thrown.

Jack slammed a punch into Matthew's gut. Matthew drifted back, dodged Jack's follow up attack and reached for a decorative plate on the wall cabinet.

"No," shouted Marion as she ran towards them. "Stop it!"

Marion grabbed Matthew's arm causing him to drop the plate. Jack pushed into Matthew and used his arm to push Marion away.

Jack surged forward and struck Matthew across the face, sending him reeling into the sideboard. A vase toppled, shattering like glass bones. Marion screamed, her voice piercing the tension. She tried to intervene, but in the flurry of limbs and curses, Matthew struck her—a sharp backhand that sent her sprawling to the floor.

Jack roared, unchained. He landed another blow, splitting Matthew's lip, blood spilling onto his collar.

Marion groaned, sitting up slowly. "I'm fine," she rasped, wiping blood from her mouth. "I'm tougher than I look."

Jack stood over Matthew, seething. "If you ever touch my wife again, your sister won't be the only dead body in this house tonight. I'm getting the police."

As Jack turned, Matthew darted for the front door.

"Don't let him get away!" Uriah cried, but his voice was a ghost of its former self, barely rising over the sobs that consumed him. Jack chased after him.

Marion walked out of the dining room as Uriah stayed on the floor. He was still in shock over what had transpired, so was Marion.

By the time Marion reached the parlor, Matthew and Jack were gone. She suddenly heard footsteps coming from above.

Marion turned and saw Mabel hurriedly coming down the stairs, still in her dress from the night before.

"What's going on? I thought I heard something break," Mabel asked.

Marion sighed. The more Marion looked at her friend's scared face the more she wondered if she could tell her the truth. It would break her heart for sure. Marion inhaled and nodded firmly. She had to tell her. It was just a matter of how she would tell her.

Suddenly, the sound of feet walking across the floorboard could be heard. Mabel and Marion froze just staring up.

Marion asked absentmindedly, "Winston is already better?"

"No," Mabel responded. "Winston's still in bed. That can't be him."

Marion raised her eyebrows in curiosity. The sound of the footsteps got louder, as if they were coming closer.

Mabel turned to the library, which was located down the hall from where Marion was standing, and gasped. She grew pale and her face became devoid of expression. Marion turned to see what had led Mabel to be in such disbelief. When she turned, she gasped as well and stared in awe.

There, standing in the doorway of the library, stood Abigail. It was an astonishingly unbelievable sight. The top of her dress was covered in dried blood. As she was framed in the doorway, she looked like a ghost, clearly distressed. Tears streamed from her eyes, but the fact that was most important about this couldn't be dismissed – Abigail Brown was alive.

Abigail shifted from side to side in a faint cry, "Somebody, please help me."

At that moment, Abigail collapsed. Mabel descended the staircase and ran to her, embracing her tightly. Marion immediately followed.

Abigail slumped into Mabel's body. Uncontrollable tears of joy and relief streamed from Mabel's face.

"Abigail! Abigail! Thank you, Lord! Thank you! Oh, God is good!" Mabel shouted, crying hysterically.

"Let's get her up," Marion suggested. Marion grabbed one arm while Mabel lifted Abigail up with the other arm. They carried her with a struggle to her bedroom upstairs.

Once in the room, they laid Abigail on the bed. Marion lifted herself up, breathing heavily. Her arms creaked and there was a slight ache, but nothing to complain about extensively. Marion was more concerned about Abigail and her condition.

Marion turned to Mabel. "I'll retrieve Dr. Ritter."

Marion turned and swiftly ran to the house next door. Once she reached outside, the morning sun spread over her.

It had been a long night. She didn't know so much time had passed. She cut between two people walking down the sidewalk and spun as she grabbed hold of the rail of Dr. Ritter's home. She ran up the steps and knocked hastily.

The door opened to reveal Dr. Ritter. His eyes widened to see Marion.

Marion wasted no time. "Come quick!"

He needed nothing more as he ran back inside and, after several long agonizing seconds, he burst through the open door. He closed the door of his home and they were soon back at the home of the Browns.

Marion led the way as she and Dr. Ritter ran upstairs to Abigail's bedroom. Dr. Ritter froze in shock to see Abigail breathing hard and wincing from the pain.

Marion was stalled by another sight that was equally as shocking. Uriah was in the middle of the room, staring stupefied at Abigail.

Abigail reached out towards Uriah as Dr. Ritter stepped forward. Marion grabbed Uriah's arm.

Uriah looked back. His face wet with fresh tears. Marion shook her head at him. Uriah looked disappointed, but he understood. He turned his back as Marion came forward.

Abigail's face widened in shock at Uriah turning on her. Marion knew it was for the best.

Dr. Ritter removed a piece of Abigail's shirt and examined the brutal lacerations.

Mabel shrunk back with her hand over her mouth.

Marion looked at Dr. Ritter.

His eyes narrowed.

"Shallow..." Dr. Ritter said as he examined her.

"What?" Mabel asked.

Dr. Ritter touched the side of one of Abigail's cuts. "These puncture wounds are rather

289

shallow. There might be hope yet...where is Matthew?"

Marion answered, "Not here."

Dr. Ritter sighed. He immediately went into his bag and retrieved some instruments. He moved with both speed and tact.

He dampened the end of one cloth and wiped Abigail's chest wounds. She winced in pain, but Mabel held her down.

"Stay calm, baby," said Mabel, reassuring her. "Everything's going to be alright."

Dr. Ritter applied a creamy balm and thick, white bandages onto each cut.

He then took out a heavy threaded cloth. He forced her into an upright position. Marion held Abigail as Dr. Ritter finished mending her wounds.

Abigail laid back down and Dr. Ritter exhaled. Mabel and Marion stared up at him.

Abigail squinted her eyes and tried to keep them open. Her breathing became slower. Marion asked, unsure if everything was okay, "Will she live?"

Dr. Ritter sighed.

"She's lost a lot of blood. Even though the wounds are shallow, there are a lot of them. I worry about possible internal damage. Any of them could be infected, too... She will need a long rest, but we will need to watch her. Mabel could you get her some water, please."

Mabel left and went to go retrieve the water. By the time she arrived, Abigail was almost asleep. Her eyes closed and her face was so gentle.

Mabel did her best to keep her awake by patting Abigail on the face. Abigail eagerly drank most of the water.

"How was she unconscious all this time?" Dr. Ritter asked.

That was a good question. Dr. Ritter rubbed his chin in confusion. He let his hand fall from his chin and began looking at her head when Uriah spoke. "Chloroform."

Marion, Mabel and Dr. Ritter turned to Uriah, who was now slumped in a chair on the other side of the room. He looked at the floor in shame. His eyes were devoid of any redemption. Marion wanted to believe something was there.

291

Dr. Ritter spoke with a serious edge as he got up. "Chloroform...that is a dangerous substance. It can, through inhalation, lead to someone falling unconscious. Uriah, how, no, what have you done?"

Uriah started to cry. Mabel's face shifted from curiosity to horror. Marion sighed. "Tell them the truth, Uriah." He struggled at first, but he quickly let it out.

"I tried to kill her. I'm sorry," Uriah said. Mabel was speechless.

"What?" she said. She turned to Marion. "What do you know about this?"

Marion looked Mabel square in the eyes.

"Jack was told by the detective that the killer was likely in the house at the time. It wasn't an intruder who attacked Abigail. It was one of our own. Jack and I decided to do our best to investigate and soon discovered that Uriah was hired by..."

Marion paused. She sighed and finally spoke, "Uriah was hired by Matthew to kill Abigail."

Mabel stared, dumbfounded. Dr. Ritter was shocked as well.

Abigail began to weep. Mabel was stunned. She quickly turned to Marion and asked, "Well, where is Matthew?"

CHAPTER 17

JACK

The city woke slowly, unsure of whether to greet the day or turn its face back to dreams. The sun crept over the skyline like an old friend returning after years of silence, spreading golden light that touched rooftops and crept down the cobblestone streets with reverent caution. The air was thick with the stillness that came before the true stirrings of life — storekeepers sweeping stoops, the metallic clink of milk bottles echoing down alleys, the half-hearted cries of newspaper boys reciting headlines even they didn't quite believe. The world was moving again, but not for Matthew.

He was still running.

Down the sidewalk he tore, his feet pounding against the earth with desperate, uneven rhythm, dodging carts and vendors and startled morning walkers. His breath came in jagged, uneven bursts, each gasp slicing his lungs open, but he didn't stop. Couldn't stop. His eyes — wild, hunted — darted from alleyways to open streets, looking for a path, an escape, something that resembled salvation.

Behind him, Jack's voice rang out — low, commanding, and furious. "Matthew, stop!"

But there was no stopping anymore. Not after what had happened. Not now that Abigail was alive. Not when the truth — sharp, hot, and relentless — was gaining on him like a hound. He pushed harder, legs screaming, vision narrowing to a tunnel of movement and light and sound. He glanced over his shoulder, just once, to gauge the distance.

And that's when it all began to fall apart.

The mounted officer came out of nowhere — just a blur of blue and brown and hooves — and the shrill whistle split the air like lightning. "Stop right there!" the officer barked, spurring the horse forward, its hooves clattering on the stone with bone-jarring speed.

Matthew cursed, breath tearing from his throat as he forced his body to move faster, pain pulsing through every limb. The city spun around him — metal, glass, noise, color — all of it a blur of motion as he chased his own vanishing freedom.

Behind him, Jack faltered. The older man bent double, gasping for breath, one hand gripping his knee as he watched in horror. "Oh no..." he muttered, his voice swallowed by the chaos as Matthew neared the intersection.

From up ahead came the warning.

The sound of a streetcar — louder now, closing in fast. The clang of its bell once. Twice. A third time — urgently, furiously. But Matthew wasn't listening. He was too busy checking behind him, watching the officer slow, misjudging the danger ahead.

For just a heartbeat, relief flickered across his face. Then he turned forward. And time ended.

The streetcar roared into view, steel wheels shrieking on the tracks, a monstrous mass of momentum that could not be stopped. Its headlights caught Matthew in full— just a boy again, eyes wide, mouth open, frozen on the edge of fate.

There was no time for a scream. Only a flash of light.

The sound of metal crashing against flesh. A cry — sharp, brief, final.

And then, silence. Matthew Brown was dead.

Later, back at the house, the morning light had reached the foyer, pouring through the open door like a slow confession. Jack stood there in its glow, unmoving, his silhouette framed by the sun's unforgiving brilliance. His expression was hollow — his eyes glazed, his mouth parted slightly — as though grief had cracked him open and left him hollow. The rage, the pursuit, the words— they were all gone now. He didn't blink. Didn't speak. He simply stood there, listening to the distant sound of screams drifting in from the street.

Inside the house, time had slowed to a crawl.

Abigail lay nestled in her mother's arms. She was in her own bedroom now. Her breathing was shallow, wet, fragile — each inhalation a victory, each exhale a question. Mabel rocked her gently, whispering prayers and lullabies half-remembered from Abigail's childhood, her tears flowing freely, caught somewhere between hope and the terror of losing her all over again.

Marion remained kneeling, her hand never leaving Abigail's wrist, feeling the faint, persistent pulse beneath her fingers — the small, stubborn beat of life that had refused to give in. Her eyes slowly drifted to Jack, still frozen in the doorway.

He didn't move.

He couldn't.

Because everything had changed.

One year later, the soft, amber light of morning filtered through the gauzy white curtains that hung delicately at the windows of the Franklin apartment, casting warm, dappled patterns on the floor and walls. The rising sun, slow and unhurried, bathed the room in gold, washing over the simple furnishings, the scuffed wooden floorboards, the worn edges of the bookshelf, the fraying threads of the old armchair in the corner — each detail speaking not of neglect but of a life lived, of moments layered like the fibers of a well-loved quilt. Outside, the world was waking gently. Birds called out their jubilant songs in bursts of melody that drifted in on the breeze, mingling with the sweet scent of dew-drenched grass and blooming magnolia, the air itself heavy with the breath of spring and new beginnings.

Inside the apartment, there was a silence that felt sacred, not empty. A silence earned, preserved, and finally welcomed.

Marion stepped out of the bedroom, her hands tightening the sash of her pale cotton robe, her bare feet whispering against the smooth, timeworn floor. Her movements were unhurried, unburdened by the frantic energy that had once defined so much of her. The hallway she crossed now had seen years of tension, arguments, rushed goodbyes, breathless returns — but this morning, it felt still, full, complete. Behind her, the bedroom door remained ajar, and through the narrow opening, Jack could be seen bending slightly at the waist, smoothing the bedspread with a kind of practiced tenderness. Each movement was slow, deliberate, almost

299

reverent—as if folding back the creases of memory itself. There was a quiet strength in him now, a softness that had not come easily, but through fire and grief, through nights of uncertainty and long days shadowed by fear.

The sun's rays stretched long and golden toward the far corner of the room, where a small wooden crib rested beneath the open window. The crib was simple, handcrafted, the kind that creaked gently when touched and bore the faint scent of pine and lullabies. There, nestled among soft, pale linens, lay a tiny form wrapped in blankets. The infant stirred—a twitch of a hand, a shift of breath, a sleepy coo too delicate to disturb the morning hush.

Marion approached quietly, her heart tightening in that strange way it did now whenever she looked at the baby. It was not just maternal instinct, not merely affection—it was something deeper, something rooted in the marrow of her bones. She leaned over, her fingers brushing the child's cheek, and then, with the gentlest motion, she gathered the baby into her arms, the warmth of the tiny body seeping instantly into her skin. The child nuzzled against her, emitting a soft sigh that fluttered like a moth's wing against her collarbone.

Her eyes closed for a moment, the weight of the baby grounding her, anchoring her to this moment, this breath, this morning. Her lips parted with the faintest of smiles — tender, fragile, radiant with the quiet joy that grows only in the aftermath of sorrow. The kind of smile that remembered loss, that bore the echo of screams and sleepless nights, but chose to bloom anyway. She inhaled slowly, deeply, letting the faint scent of milk and lavender and new life wash over her.

In this life, we embark on different paths, she thought. Some stretch forward with promise, paved in laughter and warmth. Others twist through shadow and ruin, breaking us in places we never expected. But even pain, when endured with love, gives way to light. Even grief, when shared, opens the door to grace.

Behind her, the bedroom floor creaked softly. Jack stepped into view, his silhouette framed by the morning light, the edges of his flannel shirt glowing faintly golden. He crossed the room without speaking, his eyes on Marion, on the baby in her arms. When he reached her side, he placed one hand lightly at her waist, the other gently brushing back a loose strand of her hair before settling against her back. Their bodies leaned into each other, not out of exhaustion or need, but out of instinct— two pieces drawn together by shared experience, mutual healing, and something even older than that - choice.

Together, they looked down at the child they had come to love, the child who had arrived not as an answer to their questions, but as something even more profound—a beginning they hadn't known they were waiting for.

In that stillness, something settled. A chapter closed not with the slam of a door, but with a sigh. A letting go. A welcoming in.

They stood there for what felt like eternity and no time at all, wrapped in morning light, in each other's arms, in the hush of a home that had finally known peace. And in that silence, something sacred lived—not just family born of blood, not just survival through shared history, but the deeper, harder thing.

Love, shaped not by ease, but by fire. Healing, built one breath at a time.

Hope, not naive, but fiercely earned.

And life—quiet, fragile, extraordinary life— held tenderly in the arms of those who had learned, at last, how to hold on.

In a prison yard in a rural part of the Georgia terrain, the sun bore down like a curse, unyielding in its fury, turning the clay-red earth to scorched stone. The sky was bleached white with heat, no clouds in sight—only that cruel, relentless orb burning high above the penitentiary grounds.

The yard stretched wide and hopeless, hemmed in by towering fences laced with coils of rusted barbed wire that trembled in the breeze like claws waiting to tear the sky open. At every corner and elevation, white guards kept watch from wooden towers, rifles glinting under the sun even when held in lazy, familiar poses. Sweat trickled down their necks and stained the collars of their wide-brimmed hats, but they didn't shift. They watched.

Below them, the men worked.

A long chain of Black prisoners moved with mechanical obedience, bent over under the weight of labor and sun, their striped uniforms clinging to sweat-slick skin. Shovels scraped against packed dirt, the sound rhythmic and hollow—punctuated by the soft clink of chains that bound them ankle to ankle. The yard echoed with that cruel music, a metronome of captivity.

303

Among them was Uriah Oliver.

Once, his face had known softness—an innocence shaded by hope or fear, perhaps even both. But time had carved the boyishness away, sculpting something gaunter, sharper, wearier. His cheeks were sunken now, his eyes dark and distant, dulled by repetition and memory. He moved like a man only half-alive—his limbs obeyed, but his spirit dragged behind, tethered to something no shackle could explain.

The chain around his ankle clanked with each step, linking him to the next man, and the next, and the next— souls bound in shared punishment, each carrying their own silence. Uriah's hands trembled as he dug, though not entirely from exhaustion. His fingers clutched the wooden handle of the shovel like it might keep him from falling into the earth. His lips moved in a whisper— prayer or confession, none could say—spoken to the empty sky that refused to answer.

Near the post, two guards leaned in the shade, idle and indifferent.

"What's he in for?" one asked, tipping his chin lazily in Uriah's direction.

The other squinted, spitting a stream of tobacco juice into the dirt.

"Attempted murder," he said.

But Uriah didn't flinch. Whether he heard or not, he gave no sign. His shovel kept moving — dig, lift, dump. A rhythm as relentless as the sun. He didn't look up. He didn't look around.

And the chain clinked on.

Meanwhile, in The Hilltop Graveyard, the hill was still. Not the silence of peace — but of aftermath. The whisper of pine needles drifted through the air, mingling with the faint rustle of early autumn leaves. Summer's heat had finally loosened its grip on the Georgia sky, leaving behind a cooler wind that stirred the edges of black veils and wool coats.

Three figures stood by the newly turned soil. The grave was fresh, its edges raw, the tombstone pale and unweathered. The inscription was stark, unforgiving:

MATTHEW BROWN

Brother and Son

1886 – 1911

Mabel Brown held a lace handkerchief to her mouth, trying to stifle the tremor in her breath. Her shoulders shook in spite of the shawl around them, her eyes swollen from days without rest and nights drowned in mourning. The lines of motherhood and loss cut deeper now, aging her far beyond the year that had passed.

Beside her stood Winston — rigid, composed, a still pillar of presence. His hand lay gently on Abigail's shoulder, as if anchoring her to the earth beneath them.

Abigail. Alive.

Her skin was almost translucent, like light had only just begun to return to her. A bandage, thin but undeniable, peeked from beneath the collar of her dark dress. Her hands were locked together tightly. She said nothing. But her tears spoke — the kind that didn't fall in storms, but in single drops that scarred the skin on the way down.

She stared at the name carved in stone and knew it could have been hers.

Though the chloroform had silenced Abigail, and the blade had left its mark, it had not found her heart. Like Lazarus, she had risen. Spared. A miracle, if ever there was one.

CHAPTER 18

MARION

The bells tolled sharply across the skyline of Atlanta, their chime not merely marking the hour but slicing through the morning like blades of proclamation. Each metallic note rang with a cold precision, reverberating through the concrete arteries of the city, announcing itself above the chaos of traffic, commerce, and conversation. It was a sound that demanded reverence, a sound that reminded all within earshot that time marched on— relentless and indiscriminate.

At the epicenter of that sonic call stood the cathedral — a stone-clad monolith of Gothic resilience nestled amid glass towers and modern steel. Its arches reached skyward like pleading hands, its rose window catching the sunlight and throwing fragments of color onto the street below. Inside, the air was thick with incense and history. Dust motes danced like spirits through shafts of stained glass light, casting hues of ruby, sapphire, and gold over the polished wood of the pews.

High in the pulpit, Reverend John Meadows stood cloaked in crimson vestments, the rich folds of fabric cascading over his frame like blood woven into silk. He was not a man of mild gestures or measured speech. No, his words cracked like thunder as they rolled through the nave — each syllable sharpened by years of sermonizing, each phrase carved with rhetorical precision. He spoke of sin with the certainty of one who had mapped its every contour, of redemption with the fervor of one who feared it might yet elude him, and of salvation as if he were its gatekeeper and judge.

The congregation, a sea of only White, expectant faces turned upward in ritual obedience, absorbed his sermon with rapt attention. They nodded, whispered "amen," and let his voice wash over them like a tide of absolution.

And yet, behind the fire in his speech, behind the choreography of the liturgy, there was something dissonant. His eyes — those sharp, restless eyes — betrayed him. They flitted across the room with surgical calculation, not in search of inspiration but of danger. Not to embrace, but to isolate. As if somewhere within this sanctified place sat a threat cloaked in faith. As if his very presence at the pulpit was a shield as much as it was a stage.

Elsewhere, nestled in the gentle cradle of the Georgia pines, where the sun filtered through branches like blessings whispered on the wind, sat a modest wooden cabin. Its planks, weathered and silvered with age, told stories in every grain — stories of births and storms and quiet winters by the hearth.

Inside, the air pulsed with life. The scent of lavender and sage clung to the walls, mingling with sweat and woodsmoke and the metallic tang of new blood. In the bedroom, Sarah Stevens moved with the calm precision of a seasoned midwife. Her hands — strong, scarred, and certain—guided the miracle before her with a quiet reverence. She leaned over the laboring mother, her voice low and reassuring, her presence a pillar amid the chaos of pain and possibility.

The child's cry came not all at once, but in stages— a gurgle, then a gasp, then a wail that filled the room with holy defiance. Sarah caught the newborn in a clean cloth, smiling through tears, her chest rising with a mix of exhaustion and awe. New life had entered the world, as fragile and full as the first breath of dawn.

Outside, the porch creaked gently beneath the weight of George Stevens, who rocked in his chair as if keeping time with the earth itself. Next to him sat the father of the child, laughing softly, both men sharing a silence steeped in pride and pipe smoke. Their laughter, low and knowing, curled into the air and drifted lazily into the golden canopy above.

In the heart of the town stood the dry goods store, where commerce and gossip flowed together in equal measure. The scent of burlap, peppercorn, and sun-warmed wood filled the aisles. Barrels brimmed with flour and beans, and bolts of fabric leaned like soldiers along the walls.

The din of quiet conversation fell to near silence as Albert Oliver entered.

He moved not with arrogance, but with the undeniable gravity of a man who had survived much and owed no explanation. His cane tapped a steady rhythm on the plank floor, each click a metronome of endurance, each step a declaration of dignity. He did not look left or right—he did not need to. The room bent around him, not in fear, but in unspoken recognition.

Behind him trailed whispers—not loud, but sharp. Familiar names paired with unfamiliar tones. Jealousy. Resentment. But Albert paid them no mind. They were background noise, the petty hum of those whose worlds had been too small for too long.

One man, young and reckless, stepped into Albert's path. Whether by chance or design, it didn't matter. He had made fun of Albert because of his cane. However, soon enough, the young man's foot caught on the edge of a sack, and he tumbled forward, arms flailing, pride scattering like spilled grain.

Albert neither paused nor offered a hand. His gaze flicked toward the young man, unamused, unimpressed. Then, with the ghost of a smirk, he

312

turned the corner, his cane striking once more —
clean, sharp, unforgiving.

At Spelman College, light poured into the
classrooms like hope made visible. It bathed the
desks and chairs in a gentle glow, warming
pages, softening shadows. Mary Hart sat in the
second row, her hand a blur of motion as her pen
scrawled across her notebook, thoughts
outpacing ink.

Around her, other young women whispered
dreams too big for whispers — ideas blooming
like wildflowers in fertile soil. There was
laughter, there were arguments, there were
moments of silence so electric they seemed to
hum.

Across the city, inside the halls of Atlanta
Baptist College, which would transform into
Morehouse College in the year 1913, Jim Moore
raised his hand — not out of formality, but
conviction. His eyes burned not with rebellion,
but with purpose. When he spoke, it was not
simply to answer, but to stake a claim. He did not
yet know what future awaited him, only that it
would not come quietly, and he would not go
unnoticed.

EPILOGUE

It was not a cathedral, and it did not need to be. The little church, nestled between ordinary buildings on Auburn Avenue, glowed with something eternal.

The stained glass was modest, the pews worn smooth from years of faithful bodies, and yet the spirit within the room was fierce, joyful, and rooted.

Marion and Jack stood at the front, robed in white, cradling the child they had brought into the world. The baby blinked up at her, eyes wide and impossibly bright, a life still untouched by time.

Jack stood beside her, his arm warm against her back, his gaze fixed on their son, Jack Jr., with a kind of awe that turned men to stone and prayers to fire.

The minister, gray-haired and steady, dipped his fingers into the baptismal basin. "I now baptize this child," he said gently, "in the name of the Father, the Son, and the Holy Ghost."

Water touched the child's forehead—a moment so brief, and yet eternal. The baby squirmed, wrinkled his tiny nose, and blinked as if seeing the world anew. The congregation responded not with solemnity, but with laughter and applause—light breaking through ceremony like sun through clouds.

Marion pressed a kiss to the child's brow. Jack leaned in, brushing his temple with lips made soft by reverence.

In the pews before them sat their village— Sarah and George beaming, Abigail calm and strong beside her mother Mabel, Albert upright as ever. Jim and Mary were present as well, gazing toward a shared horizon.

And in the back, cloaked not in crimson but humility, sat Reverend Meadows, quiet and still, his eyes softened by something unspoken.

The choir lifted their voices, the ceiling trembled with harmony, and Marion gazed down at the child once more. Water shimmered

315

on the baby's skin, catching the light like a blessing.

Marion and Jack looked at one another, grateful for their new chance at happiness. After all, this was not Pennsylvania Avenue, nor was it Fifth Avenue. This was an avenue of another kind. This was Auburn Avenue.

ABOUT THE AUTHOR

DOMINIQUE LANGSTON JORDAN is the author of Auburn Avenue and other books. In his spare time, he loves binge-watching Netflix, studying random historical facts, and encouraging others. He has always loved the craft of writing. Knowing that lives can be greatly impacted by a few carefully chosen words in a book, article, etc, is truly a wonderful thing!

You can subscribe to the newsletter for the latest updates at www.DLJordanBooks.com.

www.ingramcontent.com/pod-product-compliance
Lightning Source LLC
Chambersburg PA
CBHW020337180626
46812CB00001B/239